FALLING FOR YOU

RACHEL HANNA

CHAPTER 1

*J*ackson Parker strummed his expensive pen on the solid mahogany desk and growled through gritted teeth. His cell phone on speaker mode, he took a deep breath.

"Look, Donald, I don't understand the hold up. This deal was supposed to close last Tuesday. My clients aren't going to continue sitting around waiting for your sellers to get their asses in gear. You hear me? Enough's enough. That appraisal needs to be done today or we walk."

He sat back in his chair and ran his fingers through his thick black hair, the typical Parker family trait. All except for Aaron, of course; the only blond one of the siblings, he was constantly kidded about being the milkman's baby.

"Everything okay, boss?" Jackson's assistant, Mark Tyner, asked. He was a scrawny, newly graduated kid he'd hired just last year, but he was doing a good job so far.

"Just the Milton deal; People are nuts this time of year. Say, when are you heading back to Virginia for Thanksgiving?"

"Well, I was hoping to talk to you about that. I know I had promised to leave the day before Thanksgiving, but my whole family is planning a get together on the Sunday before..."

"Relax, Mark. You're welcome to leave earlier. I'll be here working, as usual," Jackson said with a sigh as he started sorting through contract paperwork again. Work was the one constant in Jackson's life.

"Aren't you going home at all? I mean, your whole family is there, right?" Mark asked, sitting down in the cushy chair in front of Jackson's desk.

"I just have too much to do right now. I've got the Milton deal, that crazy land deal with Clayton Barnes and then don't forget the new development over on Riverside. I can't take off for both Thanksgiving and Christmas this year."

"But everyone will be closed, boss. You deserve a few days..."

"Mark," Jackson said staring into the young man's eyes with his steely gaze. "Enough. Okay?"

"Yes, sir," Mark said standing up slowly and walking out of the office. Jackson wasn't normally so pointed with him, but he wasn't in any mood for people's opinions today. He'd just gotten through with his latest fling with an opinionated woman named Roma. An Italian beauty queen who had recently relocated to Atlanta for modeling work, Roma was too fussy and whiny. He couldn't stand a whiny woman, and she took whining to a whole new level. In fact, if whining was an Olympic sport, she would most certainly win a gold medal.

After three months, their so-called relationship was over. And truthfully, Jackson didn't care much. He knew when he met her that she wasn't his soul mate or future wife or any other stereotypical romantic notion. She was just one more woman in a long line of women that he wined and dined and wasted time with.

Jackson Parker wasn't your typical man. The oldest of the Parker kids from January Cove, he was known as the stand-in father of his four younger siblings. The strong, solid type, he'd remained in January Cove until his siblings were older to help his mother, Adele, care for them.

Widowed with five young children, Adele had struggled to build up a successful real estate business in January Cove. Jackson became the man of the family at thirteen years old and didn't get to leave January Cove until he was twenty nine years old. It wasn't like his mother had forced him to stay, but Jackson had always taken his responsibilities very seriously. He remembered his father, who died in a car accident, very well and wanted to make him proud. Not having a father to grow up with had been hard, and Jackson tried to do the best job he could as a stand-in for his father.

He loved his family, but sometimes going home reminded him of things he'd rather forget like not having a woman to share his life with. Sure, he'd dated lots of women in Atlanta, but no one seemed to "fit". Most were like him - career go-getters with little time to spend "dating". He wanted a certain kind of woman, but he couldn't for the life of him figure out what kind she was. And yet there was a part of him that never wanted to settle down and have a quiet family life. He was conflicted, and that irritated him to no end. In every other area of his life, he had a decisive personality, but relationships with women confounded him.

Lost in thought as he flipped through papers, Jackson almost didn't hear his cell phone ringing.

"Hello?" he said a little too gruffly.

"What crawled up your butt and died?" his brother, Kyle, said on the other end. Jackson had to laugh. Brothers had a tendency to bring each other right back down to Earth with a thud.

"Bro, what's up? I'm knee deep in real estate crap today." If anyone understood, it would be Kyle who was successful as a real estate investor back in January Cove.

"Is there ever a day where you aren't knee deep in it?"

"Not really. So what do you need?" Jackson said, still distracted by the papers on his desk.

"You gotta come home for Thanksgiving."

"And why is that?" Jackson asked sighing as he leaned back and rubbed the bridge of his nose.

"Because we're family, and you need to come home. Take a break. You're going to have a heart attack, old man," Kyle said laughing. Although Jackson was only three years older than Kyle, he seemed older than his years. Responsibility can do that to a person.

"Can't, man. I'm coming at Christmas."

"Can't or won't?"

"Both."

"Jackson, you own the freaking company. Your staff will be off. Attorneys' offices will be closed. Clients will be with their own families. There isn't one damn reason why you can't come home." Kyle was getting more than a little irritated at his brother.

"Why is this so important?"

"Because I thought you'd want to spend as much time with Mom as you could after her medical scare, that's why. Jeez, man, there are more important things than working, ya know?" Kyle was referring to his mother's recent mild stroke, and Jackson had come into town for a short time when that happened during the early summer. Although Adele was in picture perfect health now, Jackson had to admit that he was more than a little worried about her. After all, time stops for no one, and she was getting older just like anyone else.

"Don't you try to guilt me, Kyle," Jackson snapped.

"If you feel guilt, that's on you," Kyle snapped back. "Plus, if you come home, you'll get to meet Aaron's new love, Tessa. She's great, man." Jackson's stomach felt nauseous. Did his brothers really think he wanted to hear all about their fantastic love lives with amazing women? He was glad for them, but love wasn't on his horizon apparently. Sex, yes. He could get that easy enough. He had money and good looks, but when morning came those women meant nothing to him. He couldn't even relate to the feelings his brothers had for these women - Jenna and Tessa. What did that kind of love feel like?

"Fine. I'll come home for a few days, but then I have to get back. If I'm not here..."

"Yes, I know, the world will come to an end," Kyle said laughing. "See you next week."

REBECCA EVANS PULLED her curly red hair back in a ponytail and wiped down the counters at her coffee shop. It seemed like the latte machine was screwing up again and causing the contents to leak a little more than she would've liked. But, unfortunately, she didn't have the funds to fix the machine yet again. After all, she had only owned the coffee shop for a few months, and she wasn't even breaking even yet.

A single mother of a fourteen-year-old boy, Rebecca had recently relocated to January Cove in early spring. Looking for something totally new to do with her life, she had taken all of her savings and bought the old coffee shop on the corner of Main Street. It was a popular place for local residents to go, but she was still trying to make a profit on the purchase. Thinking ahead with her marketing skills, she had added entertainment on Friday nights in the form of local musicians who played guitar and sang. She had also added Wi-Fi so that local business people could work from the coffee shop during the day.

It was an old place, and she really needed to have some renovations done but that would have to wait. The coffee shop had been there for ages, even before it was popular to have coffee shops.

Working beside the beach gave her peace, and she needed that right now. Her life was anything but peaceful with an unruly teenage son to deal with every day. She understood why he was so upset all the time, but she didn't know how to fix it. She had done everything she could do to try to fix it before finally picking up and moving from New York all the way down to the small coastal town in Georgia.

He needed a fresh start. Truthfully, she needed a fresh start too. She'd been stuck in a rut for many years now, and she thought this move might push her to try something new. Live her life again. Start over.

Unfortunately, it hadn't worked out that way so far. Her son was already getting in trouble at school in their new town, and she felt more alone than ever being hundreds of miles away from what little family she had back in New York.

This certainly wasn't the way that Rebecca thought her life was going to turn out. It all started so wonderfully. She was from a close family in a small suburb outside of New York City. She grew up in an upper-middle-class family where her mother was a counselor and her father was a physician. Unfortunately, they had both died when Rebecca was only fourteen years old herself. Her father's hobby was being a private pilot of his own plane, and he had crashed with her mother on board as they headed to a medical conference in Colorado.

Rebecca had been raised after that by her aunt Mary. Her aunt was a wonderful person, but Rebecca felt lonely. She pushed herself academically and got a scholarship to a local community college and obtained a degree in marketing.

Fast forward several years and Rebecca was married with a young son when the unthinkable happened to her all over again.

She shook her head vigorously as she heard the bell ring on the front door at the coffee shop. It was times like these that she welcomed the distraction of meeting new people around town. She didn't want to think about her past anymore.

"Good morning. Welcome to Jolt," Rebecca said, forcing a smile. It just wasn't a good morning to be peppy, but she had learned that Southerners expected a proper greeting. Truth be told, being in the South had opened her up in a way she couldn't have expected. They were so welcoming to her.

"Good morning," the man said. He was handsome with dark black hair and a warm smile. "This is the first time I've been in here since you bought the place and renamed it."

"Well, thanks for stopping in," she said. "I'm Rebecca Evans." She extended her hand to shake his and he took it.

"I'm Kyle Parker."

"Parker, as in the real estate company around here?"

"Yes. My mother owns the real estate company. I'm actually a real estate investor myself," he said with a proud smile. "Nice to meet you, by the way."

"What can I get for you?"

"Just black coffee please. Oh, and two chocolate chip cookies."

"Isn't it a little early for cookies?" she asked with a chuckle as she took the cookies out of the glass case.

"They're not for me. My girlfriend and her little girl love chocolate chip cookies." Her heart fluttered for a moment at the thought of having a man who cared like that. What she wouldn't give to have that back in her life again, someone to love her, hold her, protect her. It had been so long.

"You okay?" he asked looking into her eyes concerned.

"What? Oh. Sorry. I just got lost in thought there for a moment. Your total is five dollars and fifty five cents."

He gave her a ten dollar bill and dropped two dollars into the tip jar on the counter when she handed him his change.

"How are you enjoying January Cove so far?" Kyle asked leaning against the counter.

"I love it here. It's a beautiful place to call home. Have you always lived here?" she asked as she poured his coffee and handed it to him.

"Always; I grew up here. Of course, it's a small town which means everybody knows everybody else's business."

"I can see that. I've heard all kinds of stories."

"Oh yeah? Do tell..." Kyle leaned in with his hands

on his cheeks like he was enraptured with what she was about to tell him.

"Well, let's see. I heard Delilah Smith is opening a new tea room that is going to be the talk of all January Cove. I overheard Sander Thomas saying that he and his wife are divorcing because she's cheating with Emmett Mathers..."

"Wow, you do have the scoop!" Kyle said laughing. "I like you, Rebecca. I think you'll fit right in."

"Thanks," she said with a halfhearted smile. "I hope so."

"Anyone who moves to January Cove usually has scars to heal. I don't know your situation, but I can promise you one thing."

"What's that?"

"That ocean out there will heal you. Every day, it brings something new to the shore. You just have to wait for your delivery of good luck and blessings. I'll see you around," he said with a wink and walked out the door.

Rebecca sure hoped her new friend was right. She needed good luck and blessings because she felt pretty alone right now.

CHAPTER 2

*J*ackson drove down the interstate, as he had a hundred times, but this time it felt different. It had become harder and harder to drive into January Cove. He loved his family more than anything, but he felt empty lately. He felt left behind, but he couldn't put his finger on why.

Sure, he was stubborn to a fault. He refused to let people help him. He refused to fall in love and become some sappy, lovesick man enslaved by a woman and her whims. But he couldn't help but wonder if he was the problem. At the root of every complaint he had about his life, the only commonality was him.

He took a drink of his sweet tea and adjusted the

visor to block out the bright sunlight. Turning up his music, he tried to tune out his own thoughts. Like it or not he'd always been considered the deep thinker in the family. He had to be, after all. He was the father figure to four younger kids, or at least that's how he thought of himself. He grew up faster than everyone he knew.

While his high school buddies were rolling yards with toilet paper and playing strip poker with the Callahan twins, he was babysitting and cutting the yard and learning to build tree forts. While everyone else was going to prom and experimenting with pot, he was busy earning extra money working at the dock and putting out flyers for houses that were for sale with his mother's real estate company.

He remembered those lean times. Money was so tight that he'd seen Adele go without meals more times than he could count, but he never told that to his siblings. He didn't want them to worry. He wanted to give them the stability that his father would have given them, so he shielded them from anything bad whenever he could.

It was hard to think back to the day his father died. It was a place he hardly ever went in his mind, but a long car trip into January Cove would usually bring it on. Thankfully, he only remembered parts of that day. It wasn't as if it played in his head like a movie. Instead, there were fragments that shot through his soul and heart every time he thought about it.

He was thirteen years old at the time, and he was a typical boy. He was just starting to get a deeper voice, more muscles, and hints of teenage acne on his chin. Hair was starting to grow in places he didn't expect, and his mother was constantly after him to put on more deodorant. He was an avid baseball player on the city rec team, and his father spent hours throwing the baseball with him after work in the evenings.

It was a Tuesday night like any other. His father was supposed to be home around six, like always. But six came and went, and a confused Jackson sat on the front stoop of their small home waiting and wondering. His mother was inside cooking dinner and had lost track of time until the sheriff pulled up in the driveway just before seven. The sun was going down, and Jackson would never forget the red streaked sky above the sheriff's head as he took off his hat and asked to speak with Adele.

The rest of the evening was murky in his mind. He remembered his mother screaming and falling to the kitchen floor. He recalled that her cries seemed to come from the deepest parts of her soul, and he'd never heard sounds like that before. He never wanted to hear that again. Ever.

Adele had been making his father's favorite meal, spaghetti, and Jackson had to run to turn off the meat sauce before it burned. Looking back, it was probably his first act as man of the house. Take care of mom. Take care of the kids. Make sure the house doesn't burn down.

The sheriff explained that his father had been killed in a car accident about two miles from home. Two miles. Jackson remembered hearing the sirens when they went by about an hour before the sheriff showed up. He never imagined they were for his father.

Shaking his head to release the memories, he pulled into the January Cove city limits and stopped at the pier. He had to get himself together before he got to his mother's house. He was the rock of the family, and he couldn't let them see him upset.

He walked slowly down the pier, listening to the crashing of the waves and smelling the salty ocean air. The ocean calmed him, soothed old wounds. It was a salve for his problems, but even the ocean couldn't change what his life had become lately. Always a bit of a workaholic, he'd allowed his job to take the place of everything in his life. He knew logically that he should have more. He should be more. But he felt stuck for the first time in his life.

"LEO, I just don't understand this. We moved all the way here, but your grades are still slipping. This isn't okay." Rebecca said with a sigh as her apparently disinterested son slouched in the kitchen chair beside her. "What do you have to say for yourself?"

"Nothing." Leo was the epitome of a fourteen year old boy who had lost his way. Raised without his father, he'd always ached for a man in his life. Rebecca had only dated one man, and that was only for three months. When he didn't measure up to what she used to have with Tom, she broke it off. She wondered if she would ever find a man who would love her the way Tom did.

"It's not nothing. Don't you have dreams for the future? Don't you want to make good grades and go to college?" she asked, exasperated at his lack of enthusiasm for school.

"College is for nerds."

"No it's not. What do you think you're going to do with your life if you keep getting grades like this?" She tried so hard not to push him, probably out of guilt. But she was growing tired and frustrated, and tough love seemed like a route she hadn't taken yet.

"I'll be a professional skateboarder. Or maybe a football player," he said flipping a ball of paper across the table. "Can I go now? I'm supposed to text Gina."

"Who's Gina?" Rebecca asked, alarmed that he might be getting involved with girls now.

"Relax, Mom. She's just a friend of mine who likes to play the same online game I do."

Rebecca wasn't sure she bought his answer, but she was too tired to argue.

"Leo, these grades have to come up or I'm going to start taking things, starting with that cell phone in your hand," she said sharply. Her sudden change in tone got his attention for a moment, but then he looked back down at his phone. "Did you hear me?" she asked as she grabbed the phone from his hand.

"Yes, Mom! Jeez, can we be done with this conversation now?" he growled at her. She sighed and nodded as he stood up and walked to his room, slamming the door behind him. The failed quiz and test sitting on her kitchen table made her stomach churn. He was a smart kid, but it was like he'd stopped caring. He had no direction at all, and she felt like the worst mother on the planet.

It hadn't started this way. Tom was going to be the perfect father. He was tall and strong and authoritative. Leo had only been two when his father died, but it was almost as if he'd never adjusted to life without a Dad. No one to throw the ball with. No one to explain girls to him. No one to teach him how to treat women or be a gentleman. It was one of the reasons she'd moved to the South. She had hoped that some of that supposed Southern chivalry would wear off on him.

She and Tom had had a whirlwind romance, and they had a wonderful life all planned out. Until that day; the day she couldn't think about. Every single year when the anniversary of his death came around, she found an excuse to stay home, curled up in bed. Twelve years had passed, but it didn't get any easier. She was no longer grieving Tom, but the life that she had lost that day too: the future that had been taken with him to his grave. All of her plans and hopes and dreams had vanished in an instant, and there was no one to blame or take out her anger on. She just had to forge ahead with Leo by her side, and now she wondered if she'd made so many mistakes raising him that he was scarred for life.

She walked outside of their small apartment above the coffee shop and stood on the terrace facing the ocean across the street. She breathed in the salty air and closed her eyes. Would January Cove prove to heal her and her son, or was she forever hopeless?

JACKSON DROVE through the square noticing a couple of new businesses that had opened since he was there last. The ice cream place had changed its name to Scoops, and the old coffee shop looked like it was undergoing a transformation also. He decided he needed to try it out before he left town again, but it was getting late and his mother was waiting for him.

He pulled up to her house and felt a little bit of peace for the first time in a while. There was just something about coming home again.

Before he could put his car in park, Adele came running from the house; arms open wide and a big grin on her face.

"My baby!" she squealed as he opened the door and pulled her into a long hug. Jackson was the tallest of the Parker men, and his mother was as petite as they came so he always felt like a bear squeezing a defenseless kitten when he hugged her.

"Momma," he said kissing her on top of the head. "Well, you certainly look a lot better than the last time I saw you," he said referring to her short hospital stay.

"Oh, well, you know me. I bounce back pretty quickly, son," she said smiling up at him and putting her arm around his waist. "Kyle, Aaron, come get your brother's bags. My baby's home!" she yelled to his brothers who were coming down the front steps. Both of them laughed and rolled their eyes.

"Mom's favorite son has arrived," Aaron said as he shook his brother's hand.

"Well, I am the most handsome," Jackson said with a shrug.

"I'd have to disagree on that one," Jenna said coming down the stairs. Kyle's girlfriend and her daughter had become a big part of the Parker family, and Jackson had known Jenna for years. She was like a sister to him already.

"Hey, Jenna. Good to see you again," he said hugging her and ruffling little Kaitlyn's hair. "Where's this Tessa I've been hearing about?"

"She's inside stirring the pot of chili I made," Adele said.

"Chili for Thanksgiving?" Jackson said with a laugh.

"No, silly, I'm freezing it for after Thanksgiving," Adele said. "It's turkey and all the fixings for Thanksgiving."

Aaron and Kyle grabbed Jackson's bags and headed inside while Adele took her time strolling with her oldest son. He felt guilty that she was so excited to see him. It meant that he'd failed her by not coming home more often. She was getting older, and he didn't want to have regrets about not seeing her enough.

"So, where's Addison?" Jackson asked as they made it inside. He immediately took in the sights and sounds of home. He could smell his mother's famous peach cobbler mixed with her even more famous stuffing.

Adele shook her head and sighed. "She and Jim are on a trip to Greece right now. You know that girl never stays home. I miss her so..."

"I'll have a talk with her," Jackson said under his breath. His duties as head of the family always stuck with him even though he lived hours away.

"No, honey, don't. I have a feeling something isn't right with her and Jim right now. No need to rock the boat. She'll come home when she feels the time is right. I talked to her just this morning, and she texts me all the time, but I sure would like to put my arms around all of my babies for Thanksgiving."

"You must be Jackson." He turned to see a new face standing in the living room. "I'm Tessa Reeves," she said with a smile. "And this is my son, Tyler." The adorable little boy grinned and ran into Aaron's arms. It was so strange to see his youngest brother, the boy he'd helped raise himself, holding a child that was basically his own now.

"Nice to meet you. I've heard a lot about you," Jackson said with a wink toward his little brother. "Glad you've decided to put up with this guy." He squeezed Aaron's shoulder.

"Oh, he's not so bad," she said, almost gushing with love. Jackson wondered for a moment what that might feel like to have a woman, a real woman, love him for who he was.

The next few hours were filled with laughter as everyone talked about what had been going on in their lives recently. For Jackson, it was bittersweet. He loved the interaction with his family and the women who were now going to become family, but he wished that he had something new about his life to share.

All of his stories were work related, and he was

tired of that being the only topic of conversation he could contribute. He heard about Aaron learning to be a father to Tyler and Kyle, taking Kaitlyn on her first fishing trip. All of these were memories that should be his as the oldest child in the family, but he had nothing to say.

It wasn't their fault, of course. He was so happy for all of them, but he wanted something more for himself. Maybe he had been shortsighted by spending all this time at work. In essence, he was putting his head in the sand. Now in his late thirties, he feared that the woman of his dreams had already found someone else. If he believed in the idea of soul mates, maybe his soul mate had already moved on because he had taken so long to come to his senses.

"So are you still dating that hot Italian model?" his brother Brad asked him. Brad had arrived late to the party, but that was customary for his younger brother. He was never on time for anything which was probably why he was a contractor. Weren't they always behind on something?

"No, that ended recently. I couldn't stand her whining anymore." Jackson was aware that the room got quieter as the women glared at him. "Seriously, ladies, she whined about something all the time. She was a model, and not exactly the sharpest knife in

FALLING FOR YOU

the drawer." Finally, the women started to laugh and he felt redeemed.

"Still, I wish you would settle down with someone. I worry about you being all alone up there in Atlanta," Adele said. He could tell that she was worried about him, and that was why he loved his mother so much. She truly cared about the happiness of all of her children.

"I'm fine, mother. I'm busy with my work most of the time anyway, so I don't really have a lot of time for a serious relationship right now." Jackson patted his mother's leg, but he knew she could see right through him. Yes, he was busy with work but only by choice. He had a staff of people who could do a lot of what he did every day, but it was his outlet. His escape from a life that he didn't think he would be living at this stage.

At this time of his life, he expected to be where a lot of his friends were; married, kids, family vacations, and tossing the football in the front yard with their sons. Instead, he was up to his elbows in real estate contracts most of the time with the occasional date with a woman of no real substance.

The crazy thing was that he knew a lot of men would be happy with his life. He had a great company, plenty of money and good looks. He could get women any time he wanted, but that wasn't enough for him anymore. Coming home had only driven that point even harder into his brain. He wanted to be in love like his brothers were, and the fact made him irritated with himself. He wished that he could just block it all out and not care about falling in love with some woman who was going to likely tear his world apart.

CHAPTER 3

*R*ebecca Evans opened her coffee shop the morning before Thanksgiving just like any other day. A lot of businesses in town had already closed for the holiday, but she couldn't afford to do that. Every penny counted when it came to raising her son and keeping them afloat in their tiny apartment above the coffee shop.

She was surprised when the doorbell dinged letting her know that her first customer of the day had arrived. It was her new friend, Kyle Parker, and she was happy to see him. He had given her hope that maybe living in January Cove would be the thing that turned her and her son's lives around.

"Good morning, Rebecca!" he said.

"Good morning. I'm surprised to see you here on

the day before Thanksgiving. It seems like January Cove is a ghost town today," she said walking up to the cash register.

"Yeah, people tend to close down early during the week of Thanksgiving. That's why I was glad to see you open because I definitely need a cup of coffee this morning."

"Late night last night?" she asked cocking an eyebrow upward.

"Yes, but not for the reasons you think. My girl-friend and I were at my mother's house with most of my siblings, and we tend to stay up until the wee hours of the morning laughing and talking." Rebecca felt sad inside for a moment that she didn't have a family like that to lean on. All she had was her son and her elderly aunt Mary who lived up north.

"That sounds like a lot of fun. I don't have any siblings or any family really, so I can't imagine what that must be like. How many brothers and sisters do you have?"

"One sister and three brothers. It can get pretty rowdy pretty fast," he said with a laugh. "My sister wasn't there, but my girlfriend and my brother's girl-friend were there, so that more than made up for it."

"So what can I get for you? Black coffee?" He nodded and she started making moves to get his beverage. Kyle stared at her for moment, and she turned around to find him looking at her intently. "What?" she asked with a slight smile on her face.

"What are you and your son doing for Thanksgiving?"

"Well, we are going to make some sandwiches and maybe sit on the beach." She tried not to make eye contact with him because she didn't want anyone taking pity on her and her son.

"Oh no you're not."

"Excuse me?" she said as she rang in his drink order and took his money.

"The Parker family is not about to allow our newest January Cove resident and her son to miss out on a huge family Thanksgiving."

"Listen, Kyle, I appreciate it but…'

"I won't take no for an answer. Just ask my girl-friend. I always end up getting what I want, so it's better that you don't argue with me. Besides, my mother always makes way more food than she needs to. It's like she's feeding an army."

"I don't want to impose…"

Kyle leaned into the counter and stared into her eyes. "Rebecca, this is your new start. You're going to need support in this community, so please accept my invitation. Lunch is at noon tomorrow. Here's the address," he said writing it down on a Jolt napkin.

"Thank you. We will gladly accept your invitation." She smiled at him and put the address in the pocket of her apron. "Is there anything I can bring?"

"Nope. Everything is taken care of. Consider it a nice vacation from working for a day."

With that, Kyle waved and headed back out onto the sidewalk leaving Rebecca standing there wondering how her son would react to going to Thanksgiving dinner with a huge family he'd never met before. She could only pray that he behaved himself and didn't make her look like the world's worst mother.

WHILE THE WOMEN were busy preparing the rest of Thanksgiving dinner for the next day, Jackson decided to take a walk around his old stomping grounds. He'd already been to the pier, but then he remembered that there was that new coffee shop in town. If there was one thing Jackson loved, it was a good cup of coffee.

He figured the place would probably be closed as it was the day before Thanksgiving, but he decided to give it a try. Maybe they had sandwiches or something he could eat for lunch as he was starting to get very hungry. He would have gone back home to eat, but the women had made it very clear to stay out of the kitchen or risk death by spatula.

Kyle had taken Kaitlyn out to fly her kite, and although he invited Jackson to come along, he just didn't feel like it today. He wanted to be alone and with his thoughts, which was probably a big mistake in the first place. Aaron was at the campground finishing up some last minute business before heading back over to their mother's house for Thanksgiving tomorrow. Of course Jenna and Tessa were busy helping his mother get the food prepared. And who knew what Brad was up to.

Left on his own, Jackson strolled up Main Street looking in the windows of all of the businesses he had seen since he was a child. The hardware store was still there and looked much like it did thirty years ago. The ice cream shop had changed names, but it didn't look any different inside. They still had a real soda fountain which was something you just didn't see anymore.

The ringing of his cell phone stopped him in his tracks as he strolled down memory lane, literally.

"Hello?"

"Jackson?"

"This is he. Who am I speaking with?"

"This is John Marshall. I'm the attorney in charge of the shopping center development over on Riverside."

"Oh, yes. How can I help you Mr. Marshall? I would think that you wouldn't be working as it's the day before Thanksgiving."

"Well, sometimes business matters take precedence, as I'm sure you know. I'm just calling to let you know that this deal is falling apart. Some of the permits aren't in order, and we're having zoning issues."

Jackson took a deep breath and ran his fingers through his hair, a sign of stress in the Parker family. "What? I thought everything was in order when I left town. I spoke to Susan, and she said that we were all clear on the zoning issues."

"Well, Susan isn't an attorney, now is she? She was wrong. We have some outstanding zoning issues, the appraisal still hasn't been completed, and we are having all kinds of issues with neighbors complaining to the City Council."

"So what do you want me to do?" Jackson asked exasperated.

"There's nothing we can do during the holiday,

but come Monday morning we either need to tie up these issues or the client is planning on walking away. I just wanted to let you know so that you could be mulling over any ideas."

Jackson hung up from his call with stress seeping from his pores. He felt like the wind had been sucked out of him because the Riverside deal was huge. The commission alone on the deal would carry him for months, if not pay for a full year of living expenses. He was counting on that, and the stress was getting to him. It wasn't like he didn't have other deals in the works that would support him, but he didn't want to lose the biggest one.

As he rounded the corner, he noticed that the new coffee shop, aptly named Jolt, was open. If there was one thing he needed right now, it was a nice cup of coffee. He pulled the door which activated a bell letting the employees know that he was there. However, no one came immediately. He stood there for a moment, hands in his pockets, looking around the place. It looked pretty different than the last time he'd been there when it was owned by someone else.

The countertops had been replaced, and the light fixtures looked new. It looked like the tables were the same, but there was some new artwork on the walls. It appeared that the new owner was trying to make the place more contemporary, more modern. He noticed a small stage in the corner where it appeared that musicians must set up to play.

As Jackson walked further into the coffee shop, he noticed a teenage boy sitting in a chair behind the register listening to his iPod with headphones in his ears. Jackson stood there for a moment staring at the boy who was either ignoring him or not noticing him at all. His head was bopping to the music as he played some kind of game on the iPod.

"Hello?" Jackson called. "Hello?" he said louder while standing in front of the boy.

The boy seemed to either be ignoring him or deeply engrossed in the music he was listening to.

Jackson started waving his hands to get the boy's attention, and he finally looked up. He had shaggy blonde hair and blue eyes, and he looked completely irritated that Jackson had interrupted his music. He finally popped out one of his earphones and looked at Jackson without standing up.

"Yeah?" the boy said. If there was one thing Jackson hated, it was a smart mouthed teenager. Having helped to raise his four siblings, he had been through that more times than he could count. Eye rolling, sighs and just general disrespect drove him up the wall. It was one of the reasons why he hadn't had his own children yet.

"Do you work here? Jackson asked in an irritated tone. He'd had a hard enough morning without listening to this kid give him attitude.

"Not really. My mom owns this place, but she's upstairs on a phone call."

"Well can you take my order then?" Jackson asked running his fingers through his hair. He was quickly losing patience with this kid.

"I guess," the boy said with a sigh as he took his headphones out and set them on the shelf behind him. Slowly, he stood up and made his way to the cash register as if Jackson was putting him out.

"What do you want?" he asked smacking on his piece of gum.

Jackson held his tongue because he wanted to say quite a few things, but he decided against it. After all, this kid was young and obviously not very bright if he was talking to an adult that way.

"I'll have a no foam latte with soy milk and a dash of cinnamon on top." The boy looked at Jackson and then started laughing. "Can I ask what you're laughing at?" Jackson said with his steely eyes focused on the boy.

"Yeah. It's kind of a girly drink, don't you think?"

Jackson couldn't believe the gall that this kid had. No respect for authority at all.

"I don't think it's your job to tell me what kind of drink I should have. Why don't you just ring it up and take my money, kid?" Jackson said leaning into the counter. Just then, a woman with curly red hair came down the stairs and walked up behind the boy. Jackson's first thought was how beautiful she was, but right now she looked pretty irritated.

"Is there some kind of problem?" she asked with her arms crossed.

"Actually, there is. Your cashier here has been very rude to me and I don't appreciate it."

"Rude? What has he said to you?" she asked cocking her hip out and continuing to keep her arms crossed.

"Well, for one thing he had his headphones on and completely ignored me when I came in." Jackson wasn't sure why he was complaining to this woman in the coffee shop, but he was frustrated and irritated and probably taking a little bit of that out on her.

"Well, he doesn't officially work here. This is my fourteen-year-old son," she said still keeping her arms crossed. Something about her was alluring but Jackson couldn't quite put his finger on it. He loved her curly red hair, but her attitude seemed to match her son's.

"Then I guess you shouldn't leave him down here to take care of your business. I assumed you were open and ready to take my order when I walked in," Jackson said crossing his arms to match her stance. Suddenly he felt like he was in some kind of a standoff with this perfect stranger. "He also made fun of my drink order and told me it was girly."

The woman leaned down and looked at the register tape and then giggled under her breath. "Well..." she said with a sly smile.

"What? You're laughing at my drink order too? What kind of business are you running, lady?" Jackson snapped. The look on her face changed from playful to angry very quickly.

"Sir, I really don't appreciate you coming in here and snipping at my son or me. I don't need customers like you." She stood firm with her arms still crossed and stared him in the eye. Jackson couldn't believe what he was hearing. He was one of the Parker family, the most well-known and respected family in town. Who was this woman running a tiny coffee shop to tell him that he wasn't a valued customer? And was that a Northern accent he heard?

"Well, then, I'll take my business elsewhere." Jackson said before turning around and walking toward the door. "And let me give you a little piece of advice since you seem to be new to January Cove. People don't like it when you don't offer good customer service. This is a small town and word gets around quickly. Good luck to you, ma'am," he said with a wry smile before walking out the door.

Rebecca turned around and glared at her son. "Leo, what have you done? I can't afford to let my name be mud in this town. This business is the only thing we have to support us. Were you rude to that man?"

"No, mom," Leo sighed. "I was just listening to my music and that guy had an attitude."

"Leo, seriously, you have to be alert when you're watching the register for me. If I hadn't come down here, that guy might've gotten irate with you. You have to be more responsible." She ran her fingers through her curly hair and sighed. Raising a teenage son by herself was proving to be harder than she would have ever imagined.

It didn't help that she had an attitude with the guy too. The reason she had been upstairs on the phone was because one of her friends had called from New York. Worried about Rebecca, she was trying to talk to her about coming home. Talking to her friend only reminded her of what she'd lost over the last decade.

Janine was her oldest friend in the world. They'd known each other since kindergarten and had gone through every life challenge together. But when the unthinkable happened to Rebecca twelve years ago, she just couldn't stay in the area anymore. She and her son needed a fresh start, although Leo was making it a lot harder than it needed to be. Sometimes she felt a little resentful to her son because he didn't really know what he had lost. He was far too young when his father died, but Rebecca sure remembered her late husband. She was sorry that Leo never got to know him, but she couldn't understand how the absence of a man he never knew affected him all these years later.

It still affected her. Every so often she would go through an old box and smell his cologne. Or she would see his favorite movie or hear a song that they listened to together. It seemed reminders were everywhere even though she'd moved so many miles away from home.

Talking to Janine had only frustrated her more. Her old friend couldn't understand why she had to pick up and move all these years after her husband had died. Why did she do it now, Janine wanted to know. The problem was that Rebecca didn't have an answer for that. She had gone with her gut and done what she thought was best for her and her son. Janine didn't understand it, but she was accepting of it. She just wanted to see Rebecca, and Rebecca wanted to see her too.

But the reality was that Janine had a life. She had been married for over ten years, and she and her husband were very happy. They had three small children to take care of. Even though she wanted to help Rebecca, Janine had her own life to live. Rebecca didn't want to interfere with that anymore. She didn't want to ask for help from anyone. Leo was her responsibility, and she had done what she thought was the right thing.

"Rebecca, you know if you come home I will help you. I didn't realize that Leo was giving you such trouble. Dan and I are more than happy to talk to him or help him in whatever way we can..." Janine had said.

"I really appreciate that, but he is my son to raise. Janine, as much as I miss home, we needed this fresh start."

"Don't get mad at me, but is it possible you're just

trying to run away from the past? I mean, have you told anyone there what happened to Tom?"

"Janine, I don't want to talk about this anymore. I haven't told anyone here because it's none of their business. It doesn't matter. I'm sick of people looking at me with pity in their eyes. I've done that for over a decade now."

"I don't understand. How do you ever expect to start over if you can't be honest with people about what happened to your husband? It shouldn't be a secret. Why can't you just let people support you?"

"Look, I don't have time for this right now. I have a business to run and I left Leo downstairs. I'll talk to you later." She hated hanging up on her best friend like that, but she just couldn't take any more. No one could understand the kind of pain that Tom's death brought upon Rebecca. Well, at least very few people could understand it.

CHAPTER 4

*J*ackson sat in the café across the street from Jolt and wondered about the red haired lady inside. Although their first meeting had been more of an altercation, he couldn't stop thinking about her. There was something different about her. Something deep. A sadness that played across her face, but strength unlike anything he'd ever seen. He wasn't sure what to make of her.

He also wasn't sure why he couldn't stop thinking about her. Obviously, her son was in some kind of turmoil because no normal teenager would act like that to a perfect stranger. He could feel anger in the boy, and he sort of related to it. He remembered being angry like that after his father had died, but he had no idea what the boy's background was. For all he knew, the woman might be married and the father might just be upstairs in the apartment.

"Lost in thought, brother?" Jackson hadn't even noticed Kyle walking into the café.

"What are you doing out so early?" Jackson asked kicking the chair across from him out a little bit so his brother could sit down.

"I had an early appointment, a foreclosure over on the south side. What are you doing over this way?" Kyle asked as he waved at the waitress to bring him a cup of coffee.

"Just familiarizing myself with the town again. I noticed a new coffee shop opened up and a couple of other places, so I just took a walk. Where's Jenna?"

"She just got Kaitlyn off to school. I think she had a nail appointment after that," Kyle said with a laugh. "Listen, I'm glad I ran into you. I'm getting ready to propose to Jenna soon." Kyle smiled, and Jackson was happy for him.

"Congratulations, man. It's been a long time coming," Jackson said with a smile reaching out to shake his brother's hand. "And, if you can find someone willing to marry you, you should definitely lock her down as soon as possible." Kyle laughed at his brother's jab, but there was nothing that could wipe the smile off of his face.

"Now we just have to find you Mrs. Right," Kyle said winking at his brother as he took a sip of his coffee.

"Um, no thanks. I've had enough girlfriends to last me a lifetime. There is no Mrs. Right for Jackson Parker." Jackson tried to play it off as a joke, but he was starting to believe that was true.

"I don't believe that for a minute. You might be the oldest, but I think you're the least mature when it comes to the love department." Kyle shook his head and took another sip of his coffee. "I mean, what is it with you? Why can't you stay in a serious relationship?"

"Who are you, Dr. Phil? It's none of your business, dear brother. You just focus on your love life and I'll focus on mine." Jackson was trying not to sound snippy, but he was getting a little bit aggravated.

"Or lack thereof," Kyle said rolling his eyes. "Listen; keep the engagement thing under your hat. I've got some more planning to do before I pop the question. Got to go. Running by the jewelry store across town."

Jackson waved goodbye to his brother before putting his tip money on the table and stopping by the restroom. He thought more about what Kyle had said to him, but his little brother wasn't in a position to tell him how to live his life. If there was a Mrs. Right out there for Jackson Parker, he couldn't imagine where she might be. He'd looked high and low for years, and there just didn't seem to be a woman out there who could match him. Maybe some people just aren't meant to have soul mates, he thought, as he walked outside and headed down the street toward his car.

ADELE PARKER LOVED Thanksgiving more than just about anything. Having most of her family together, she enjoyed cooking all the food and catching up on long overdue conversations. And now she had two new women in the family with Jenna and Tessa. Each of the women had brought a new strength to their family, and she was sure that her sons would be announcing wedding plans anytime now. At least she hoped so.

The one thing that was missing from this Thanksgiving was the presence of her beloved daughter Addison. She was so worried about Addison, but she didn't want to tell her sons just how worried she was. Her daughter didn't sound right on the phone anymore, as though she were keeping a secret that was too embarrassing or upsetting to tell. Adele could tell that her daughter had something going on, but she also knew that she was an adult and could make her own decisions.

The truth was that Adele had never really liked Addison's husband anyway. He seemed gruff and a little cocky. But, everybody has their own character flaws, so Adele figured that Addison must have seen something in him that she didn't. She was a mother who didn't like getting too involved in her children's business, unless she felt like she had to step in. If she could only figure out what was going on with Addison, she probably would step in which is why her daughter wasn't telling her anything.

As she rolled out the dough for the yeast rolls, Adele was lost in thought and didn't even hear Jackson walking into the kitchen.

"Mom? Are you in there?" Jackson said waving his hand in front of her face. She wasn't sure how long he'd been standing there, but she got out of her haze and turned around.

"Oh, Jackson. Sorry. I didn't see you there."

"Apparently not," Jackson said raising an eyebrow. "Are you okay?"

"Sure. Just thinking about all the things I need to make for Thanksgiving..."

"Mom, it's me. I know you better than anyone else, and something is going on. Out with it," Jackson said. He was right. He had helped her raise his siblings much like a husband would, and he knew her better than anyone else in the world. He knew her facial expressions, her tone of voice and a multitude of other pieces of body language that would tell him when something was really wrong. In fact, sometimes it made him feel guilty that he didn't live close by anymore so that he could make sure to keep an eye on his mother. Maybe that was why she had a mild stroke last summer. Maybe it was because he wasn't around enough to watch out for her. Shrugging off the guilt as best he could, Jackson went back to trying to figure out what was wrong with his mother.

"It's nothing, really. There's nothing to worry about, Jackson. I'm fine. Sometimes mothers just get lost in thought." She turned around and went back to rolling the dough for the yeast rolls, and Jackson knew for sure that something was wrong. He thought for a moment about her mention of being a mother and realized that she had to be talking about her only missing child, Addison.

"This is about Addison, isn't it?" he asked.

Adele didn't say anything or turn around, and he could see that she was hanging her head a little bit lower, a sure sign that he had hit the nail right on the head.

"Mom, turn around and look at me." he said. Adele slowly turned around, and he could tell that she had tears in her eyes. Adele was a woman who didn't cry a lot. She never had time to cry with all that she had to do to raise five children, so when she teared up he knew that she was really worried about his sister.

"Okay, fine. It's just that Addison doesn't sound right when I talk to her on the phone or even when she texts me. I feel like something might be wrong, but she's not telling me what it is. I just hope that she's okay. It worries me," she said in a whisper. She didn't want to worry the other kids or cause a darkness over Thanksgiving for everyone else.

"Don't worry, Mom, I will talk to Addison," Jackson said. He was always taking control of situations, and this was no exception.

"No, don't. Really, Jackson. I don't want her to feel like we're all talking about her behind her back."

"Okay, fine. How about I just make a normal phone call between brother and sister and see what I think? If it sounds like she's not herself, maybe I can do a little digging around in our conversation to see what's wrong. Addison and I were always close when she was growing up, so maybe she will tell me something that she hasn't told you." Adele nodded and swiped at her eyes, brushing away a stray hair that had fallen in her face. She reached out and hugged her son tightly as if she was so appreciative of his presence back in the house. Jackson felt a pang of guilt again that he hadn't been around enough in recent years.

It was like he'd escaped from his family in January Cove, but there was nothing there that was horrible. A lot of people ran away from their lives because they wanted to get away from toxic family or areas of the country that gave the bad memories, but that wasn't the case for Jackson. His sole reason for being away from home was simply that he was alone and a failure at love so far. Maybe he was jealous of his brothers' good fortune in the relationship department, or maybe being in January Cove just reminded him that he hadn't progressed very far in his personal life since he was thirteen years old.

He couldn't quite put his finger on why he'd run away. It was like he was trying to prove something to himself and everyone else. He wanted to prove that he was the most successful brother in the family since he was the oldest. He had to excel above everyone else or he would feel like a failure.

Jackson left his mother to finish up her work in the kitchen while he walked outside to the back deck. The solitude of January Cove provided him a welcome respite from the stresses of his real estate career. Suddenly, he was starting to feel like his life in Atlanta wasn't nearly as fulfilling as he pretended it was. There's something that always drew him back to his family, his home, the waters in the ocean. He had missed the smell of the salty sea air, the breeze that lightly touched his face, the small-town life where everyone knew everyone else. And now he felt conflicted in a way that he never had before.

JACKSON WOKE up on Thanksgiving morning way earlier than he'd planned. He could already hear mixers going in the kitchen, and the loud laughter of the women as they started preparing the big Thanksgiving meal. He wondered what they were talking about that was so hysterically funny at six o'clock in the morning.

Sitting up in his bed and rubbing his eyes, he

stepped out onto the hardwood floor and headed for the restroom. He put some cold water on his face, brushed his hair and threw on a T-shirt and a pair of baggy athletic shorts. Even though it was winter time, he still found January Cove to be warm enough to wear shorts in November. After all, he had been in Atlanta where it was a lot colder during this time of the year.

"Good morning, ladies," he said with his best smile. The women giggled, and his mother tried to stifle a smile. "Is something funny? Is my hair askew?" he asked pretending to fix his hair with his fingers.

"No, honey, you look lovely," his mother said ruffling his hair as Jenna and Tessa started laughing.

"Okay, ladies. I can tell that you're laughing at my expense. What's so funny?" he asked crossing his arms and shooting a sly smile their way.

"Well, your mom was just giving us the lowdown on some of your romantic adventures as a teenager," Jenna said cutting her eyes at Adele who started to laugh.

"Oh really? My dear mother is talking about my private romantic life?" Jackson said wagging his finger at his mother. "And what, pray tell, did she tell you ladies?"

"Well, there was talk about a couple of teenage girls climbing out of your window..." Tessa said wagging her finger back at him. He liked this Tessa chick. She seemed to have just enough of a rough edge to fit right in with the rest of the Parker siblings.

"Mom! I can't believe you told them that. I told you that I was just playing board games with them!" he said with his hands on his hips."

"Oh, yeah. Sure. Board games. Likely story," Jenna said rolling her eyes. "Besides, I heard one of those was a Callahan sister."

"Listen, I never had any luck with the Callahan sisters. I was too busy helping to raise my snotty little brothers and sister." His attempt at a joke seemed to fail.

A hush fell over the room for just a moment, and Jackson could tell that he had made his mother feel bad or inadequate or something. She looked at him for a brief second and then turned around and started stirring the mashed potatoes. He felt terrible. "Listen, mom, I'm going to go grab a shower and then make that phone call we talked about. Okay?"

She turned around and nodded. "Sure, honey, that would be great. Lunch is at noon, so just make sure that you are back down here by then."

He gave her a quick kiss on top of the head and then trotted back upstairs. He wasn't sure why what he said caused her to pull back so. Maybe she felt guilty that he'd had to step up after his father died. He'd always been her right hand, but he didn't know how his mother really felt about that.

Jackson got a shower, made himself a cup of coffee in his little coffeemaker upstairs and sat out on the deck for a little while. He watched traffic go by and for some reason his eyes kept getting drawn to the new coffee shop. Jolt. Even though he had an altercation with the sexy new owner, he didn't have any plans to go back to that place. Her son had a major attitude problem, and she obviously wasn't going to do anything about it. What kind of mother allowed her son to talk to people like that? She obviously wasn't a very good disciplinarian, and he could probably teach her a thing or two about that. If one of his brothers had ever talked to anyone the way that kid had talked to him, he would've smacked the snot out of them. But, this woman apparently didn't have much of a backbone.

He finished up his coffee and dug his cell phone out of his pocket. It was time to call his sister and try to figure out exactly what was going on. He had a feeling his mother was right. Addison had never pulled this far away from the family, and she rarely missed a holiday. Although she and her husband did travel quite a bit, Addison always stayed in close contact with the family. Lately, things hadn't been the same, and he could feel it himself.

"Hello?" Addison answered. Her voice sounded softer than normal, and for a moment he wondered if he'd woke her up. It was already after 9 AM, and she was usually a pretty early riser. Of course, he had no idea where she was in the world right now.

"Hey, sis. It's Jackson. Are you okay? You sound tired," he said.

"Oh, hey, Jackson. Yeah, I'm fine. Just had a late night out. You know how we like to have a good time. Slept in for a while this morning. How is everyone?"

He could tell that she was brushing his concerns off, and that just made him even more worried about her. "We're all fine. Missing you for Thanksgiving, though."

"Yeah, I really wish we could've been there. I hate missing a holiday with my Parker brothers. But, I'm going to try my best to get there for Christmas."

"I thought you guys were in Greece or some other exotic locale?" Jackson said. There was a silence on the other end of the phone for a moment as if she was trying to think of something to say.

"Um, yeah, at the last minute Jim had a change at work..." She was stuttering and stammering, and Jackson knew he had to act fast.

"Come on, Addison. You and I both know that something is going on. You would never miss a Thanksgiving with the family if you were stateside. I'm your big brother. I can help you. Please just tell me what's wrong."

Addison didn't say anything for a moment and then he heard what he thought was a sniffle on the other end. "Jackson, I'm fine," she said through what sounded like tears.

"Why won't you let us help you?" he asked. He was aware that his tone sounded like he was begging, and he really was. He wanted to help his sister. All the brothers felt that way about her being the only girl.

"There's nothing to help me with. Really. Everything is fine. I've got things under control."

"Are you okay? Are you safe? Has someone hurt you?" Jackson started rattling off questions to her.

"I'm safe. No one is hurting me, I promise. I just need to be away right now. Please don't say anything to Mom. I don't want her worried about me."

"Too late. She's very worried about you, Addison. And now that I've talked to you, I'm worried too. If something is going on with your husband, you need to let me know about it. I can help you fix this."

"Jackson," she snapped. For the first time in their phone conversation, he heard his sister getting aggravated. She was usually a pretty feisty one anyway, so he was kind of glad to hear her backbone finally. "I'm not going to say it again. Everything is fine. Nothing to worry about. I've got things handled." There was a silence between brother and sister for a few moments before Jackson finally got the message that his sister wasn't ready to talk about whatever was going on with her.

"Okay. Just know that you can call me anytime, day or night. I will be there to help you. I promise."

"I know you will. You always have been. And I thank you for that. But I really need to take care of myself right now. I hope you can understand that. And please make up something to tell mother so that she's not worried about me. I can't take the guilt of her having another stroke just because she's worried about me."

"Alright. I hate lying to Mom, but I know it's for the best in this case. I'll tell her that something came up with Jim's job, and that finances are a little tight right now. I'll just tell her that you guys are too proud to ask for money to travel, so you're staying closer to home."

"Sounds like a good cover story. That will work. Thanks, Jackson."

"And, Addison, just know that I love you," Jackson said.

"I know. And I love you too. I'll be home soon. See you at Christmas," she said with her voice cracking before she hung up. Jackson sat there for a moment wondering if there was anything else that he could do, but Addison was a grown married woman who had made her requests clear. And he understood that himself because he didn't like people interfering in his life either. But as her older brother and stand-in father for most of her life, he was used to taking care of things for his little sister. Feeling like his hands were tied, he set his cell phone down on the dresser and started to get ready for the Thanksgiving festivities.

REBECCA WASN'T sure that she had ever been more nervous in her life. It was silly really, after all that she and Leo had been through in their lives, but going to a Thanksgiving festivity with such a well-known family was making her a little more than jittery. Of course, being a coffee shop owner, she'd had more than her share of espresso this morning. That probably wasn't the best idea given the fact that she was already anxious.

"I don't get it. Why can't we just have sandwiches on the beach like we said we would?" Leo whined. Sometimes she wondered if he was two years old or fourteen years old.

"Because I'm trying to make a name for myself in this town, and my best customer invited us. So you will act right and be kind to these people. You will say thank you and you will be polite. You hear me?" she said, putting her hands on his shoulders. She really hated this part of being a parent. Sometimes she was kind and meek like her mother was, and other times she had to be rough and tough like her father was. It was a very hard balancing act. She was never really sure that she was doing it right. It was times like this that she really missed having her husband there.

"Fine. Is it time to leave yet?" he asked looking down his cell phone.

"Actually, yes it is. We're going to walk there because it's just a couple of blocks over."

"Walk? Why can't we drive a car like normal people?" he said throwing his hands up in the air.

"Because it's one of the perks of small-town life, Leo. Get over it." She was tired of being so rough on him this morning, but he had started with his whining first thing in the morning. She just didn't understand him anymore. He had gone from being a sweet young boy to a hormonal teenage mass. She sure couldn't remember acting that way to her parents, although her father never would've allowed it. Again, she felt a momentary sense of loss when she thought about her husband. How he could've changed Leo's life. Would Leo be a better kid right now if his father was still alive? Was it even his fault that he was so angry right now?

She had tried a couple of times to talk to him about his anger issues lately, but he just went inward and started playing video games or texting on his phone. Maybe every parent of a teenager went through this at some point, but she was quite sure that she had seen parents out in public with their teenagers having a good time and interacting. That had stopped with Leo over the last year or so. She missed their close relationship, but she had absolutely no idea how to get it back.

Rebecca packed up the muffins that she had

made to take to the Parker's and they headed down-stairs and out the door. Their walk was quiet, with Leo texting on his phone as usual. Honestly, some-times she thought about grabbing it out of his hands and flinging it out into traffic. Only there was no traffic in January Cove, so it wouldn't do much good. It would likely lay out in the street untouched for hours. It was a ghost town on Thanksgiving, and it wasn't busier on most days anyway.

"Leo, can you please stop texting? If you don't, I'm going to take that phone and put it in my purse for the rest of the day," she said raising an eyebrow to him as they walked. He rolled his eyes, sighed and shoved it in his pocket. The last thing he wanted to do was lose that phone, and she knew it.

"Why do you care so much what these people think anyway? They don't even know us. They don't even know our story," he said. She was shocked by him saying this, specifically the mention of "their story". What exactly did he think their story was?

"Because it's good to make new friends, Leo. This is our new beginning. I did this for you just as much as I did it for me."

"Yeah, right," he said.

"So you think I did this whole move for me? Trust me, Leo, it's very hard for someone my age to just pick up and leave everything they've known their whole life. I did this because I felt like we needed a fresh beginning somewhere without all the memories of what happened. Don't you like it here?" she asked exasperated.

"It's alright. Of course, I don't really care where we live. It's always the same."

"What do you mean?" she asked, finally excited that he seemed to be opening up. Instead, he shrugged his shoulders, grunted and stopped talking. She'd come so close to getting him to say something, anything. But he didn't. And they walked the rest of the way to the Parker's in silence.

When they arrived at the house, Rebecca felt her nerves cropping up all over again. Her palms were sweaty, and her heart was racing. What was it about hanging out with these people on such an innocuous holiday that was making her anxious? Maybe it was because she hadn't really been to any big family functions in years. She didn't really have any family, and she didn't like to impose on friends back in New York.

But this was different. They needed support, some kind of anchor in January Cove. She just needed something new, something to take her mind off her growing problems with her son and her floundering business.

"Remember, be nice," she said reminding her son by wagging her finger in his face. They walked up the steps and rang the bell, ready to have a big family Thanksgiving with a family they didn't know.

The door flung open, and a small petite blonde woman was standing there. She assumed that this was Adele Parker, the renowned real estate broker and perfect mother to the Parker kids.

"Welcome!" she said throwing her arms out and bringing Rebecca into a big hug. It took her aback because she hadn't felt the love of a mother in so many years, but Adele Parker wasn't her mother. It was a strange sensation that she couldn't place.

"Thank you for having us. I'm Rebecca Evans, and this is my son Leo." Rebecca pulled back from the hug and put her arm around her son's shoulders. Of course, Leo wiggled out from under her grasp and crossed his arms. For a moment, there was a spark of silence as Adele looked into Rebecca's eyes and then over at Leo. Rebecca was so embarrassed, but she tried to play it off and just smiled.

"Well, happy Thanksgiving. Come on in. Most of the family is already here, so let me introduce you." Adele led her and her son into the kitchen where everyone was standing around talking and laughing. Rebecca had never felt that kind of camaraderie in a family. Being an only child and losing her parents young, she had never been to big family functions. Their family was incredibly small, even when her parents were alive.

As she walked into the kitchen, her concerns were relieved when everyone welcomed her with open arms. There was no silence or strange looks being shot her way like she wasn't supposed to be there. Instead, everyone came up and either shook her hand or gave her a friendly hug. There was definitely something to be said for living in a small town. Southern hospitality at its best, she thought.

"Welcome," one of the women said. "I'm Tessa Reeves. I'm the newest member of the Parker family, I guess you could say. I'm dating Aaron, the youngest brother over there with the blonde hair." Aaron smiled at her from across the room and Tessa blew him a kiss which made it very obvious that they were newly in love.

"Oh give it a break. Gag," one of the men said. "I'm Brad. I'm one of the unattached brothers that my mother is trying to marry off." Rebecca had to laugh at that, and she immediately noticed how good-looking he was. In fact, all of the Parker men in the room were very good-looking, and Adele was a beautiful woman.

"He's just jealous that he doesn't have a woman right now," Kyle said pushing his way through the small crowd. "Listen, people, I invited Rebecca and her son so let's not show her how crazy our family really is." Everyone laughed and nodded their heads, and Rebecca felt immediately at home. "This is Jenna, my girlfriend, and her daughter Kaitlyn."

"Hi, Jenna. Hello, Kaitlyn. Very nice to meet you. I'm Rebecca and this is Leo," she said. Leo stood there with his arms crossed only nodding his head when people said hello, completely disinterested. She wanted to smack him, but she figured that probably wouldn't be the best way to introduce herself to the Parker family.

"Where's Jackson?" Kyle said looking around.

"I don't know. I know he was upstairs making a phone call and taking a shower earlier, but I haven't seen him in a couple of hours," Adele said.

"Relax, I'm coming. The life of the party is..." Jackson said as he made his way down the stairs and stopped dead in his tracks when he saw red curls from across the room. Rebecca turned around and their eyes locked, but not in a good way.

CHAPTER 5

*J*ackson felt like the breath had been completely sucked out of his lungs when he saw her. He'd had a hard time not thinking about her since yesterday, but he should have been livid. After all, she was rude to him and completely uninterested in his business.

"Rebecca, this is my brother Jackson. He lives in Atlanta, but he has graced us with his presence for the Thanksgiving holiday," Kyle said putting his arm around his brother. Jackson just stood frozen in place staring at Rebecca. She stared back, but he could tell that she was gritting her teeth as he could see her jaw clenching from across the room. Her son sighed and ran his fingers through his hair, much like Jackson did when he was stressed out.

"Rebecca. Nice to meet you," Jackson said nodding his head. Normally, he would reach out and shake someone's hand when he met them, but he didn't think his touch would be welcome to her right now. Her son, Leo, stood there with his arms crossed staring at Jackson. He could see the anger under the surface, but he wasn't altogether sure that the anger was completely related to him. The kid just seemed angry all the time.

"Nice to meet you," she said softly before turning around and looking back toward the kitchen. "Boy, something sure smells good. Adele, do I smell peach cobbler?" she said desperately trying to change the subject and get out of the foyer.

"Absolutely. It's an old family recipe. Come on, I'll show it to you." Adele took her in the kitchen and Leo just continued staring at Jackson while everyone else started to mingle again. It was like there was a silent message going back and forth between the two, and Jackson wasn't really sure what to do about it.

"Have a seat," Jackson said to Leo pointing at one of the kitchen chairs in the breakfast area.

"I don't want to sit down," Leo said crossing his arms.

"Suit yourself, but with such a big family, chairs

are hard to come by around here." Jackson shrugged his shoulders and walked past Leo into the kitchen.

Jackson watched Leo out of the corner of his eye, and the boy eventually walked over and sat down. Apparently, his mother must've told him to leave the telephone alone because he wasn't pulling it out of his pocket. He looked bored, as many teenage boys would have in that situation, but more than that he looked almost sad. Jackson wondered about it, but didn't have a lot of time to think before his mother was dragging him through the kitchen to pick up a heavy box off of one of her top shelves in the laundry room.

He should've known better when his mother asked for his help because she was up to no good.

"So what do you think?" she asked rubbing her hands together and grinning. Obviously, there was no box in the laundry room.

"What do I think about what?" Jackson asked even though he knew exactly what his mother was referring to.

"About Rebecca. Isn't she beautiful?"

"She's very nice looking, mother. But I'm not interested." Jackson turned to walk out the door, but Adele grabbed his arm.

"Why aren't you interested?" she demanded to

know. Looking down at her blue eyes, he felt sorry for her. He knew that she just wanted him to be happy, and that's what he wanted too. He just had absolutely no idea how to get there.

"Well, for one thing, I live in Atlanta and she lives here. For another thing, she has a son with anger problems and I don't need that in my life right now. For a third thing, I met her at the coffee shop the other day and we didn't exactly hit it off."

"Oh, Jackson, tell me you didn't make her feel unwelcome here." Adele shook her head and closed her eyes. Why did he feel like he was a three-year-old getting in trouble for putting his hand in the cookie jar?

"I didn't do anything. It's a long story, but suffice it to say she is not a fan of mine. She had no idea I was a Parker, and I had no idea she would show up here for Thanksgiving."

"Mom, the turkey is ready. Everybody is starving," Brad said popping his head in the laundry room door. "Did I interrupt something?" he asked with a grin. Brad was notorious for being the nosy one in the family. Most people would probably think the only girl, Addison, was the nosy one but not so in the Parker clan. Brad was always trying to find out the scoop, and they often joked that he should've been a reporter.

"No, honey, you didn't interrupt anything. Let's go have some lunch. After all, we do have guests," Adele said cutting her eyes up at her son. She walked out into the kitchen and went back to her normal self, preparing food and cutting up with the family. Jackson stayed in the laundry room for a moment so he could look at Rebecca from across the room without her thinking that he was some kind of stalker.

His mother was right about one thing. She really was a beautiful woman. He'd never seen hair that color of red before, and it was thick and curly. She had a unique look, and it was hard to take his eyes off of her. Her skin was like porcelain, and her blue eyes were crystal clear. But just like her son, she had a hint of sadness in her eyes. It was like something bad had happened to the both of them, and they were having a hard time getting their heads above water. He vowed that he would try to be kinder to her today and let their meeting yesterday be a thing of the past. He just hoped that she could do the same.

REBECCA COULDN'T BELIEVE IT. Of all the crappy luck in the world, she had to see her absolute worst customer standing there at the Thanksgiving table. And the fact that she kept catching him staring at her only made her more uncomfortable.

It was hard enough bringing her unruly teenage son to a strange house on Thanksgiving without the glare of the world's worst customer. Okay, so maybe she was overreacting a bit, but the last person she wanted to see was this man. Jackson Parker. Who knew he would be one of the Parker family? They all seemed to be so nice, but maybe he was their exception. Maybe he was the black sheep of the family.

The only problem was that he seemed very nice at the present moment. Not only that, but she was finding herself noticing just how handsome he was. The tallest of the group, he had those brooding, dark good looks that women search the world over for. But not her. She didn't have any interest in him, she told herself.

As they sat around the table, she found herself feeling more comfortable. She couldn't tell what Leo was thinking as he was being his quiet, teenage self. At least he wasn't mouthing off or saying anything offensive. She'd wanted to wash his mouth out with soap a few times in the last couple of months.

The food was great, and the conversation entertaining. The Parker family was loud, and they reminded her of those big Italian families from up north that she was so accustomed to. Even though she wasn't Italian, she sure enjoyed being around her friends' families growing up. There was always something going on, and lots of food and entertainment.

Her family was from an Irish background, but because the family was so small she never got to experience big family functions like this one. It was nice. She wondered what it would be like to have a brother or sister to share her life with, especially as lonely as she felt in the world sometimes. Being a single mother and a widow wasn't easy, and she wondered if the stress of it would ever be lifted off of her shoulders.

"So, Rebecca, where are you from originally?" Brad asked. He seemed to be a very nice guy, and very inquisitive. In fact, she had noticed that he seemed to ask more questions than anyone else at the table during the entire meal.

"I'm originally from a suburb of New York City. That's where we lived before we came here." She felt like she was giving very short answers, but she didn't really want to talk about her past today. It was hard enough every other day of the year.

"So what made you move all the way to January Cove? I mean, this is a far cry from the big city," Brad asked. Jackson looked at her intently as if he was waiting for the answer to her question, and she didn't really know how to answer it. How had she missed preparing for all of this? Surely people would want to know the answer to that, but she'd never given thought to an appropriate, politically correct answer.

"Well, we just needed a change of pace."

"Oh, mother, why do you continue to lie to people?" Leo muttered under his breath. The whole table went silent, and Rebecca could feel her heart pounding in her chest. What on earth was her son trying to do to her?

"Leo…" she said looking at him with that motherly glare that usually shuts kids up. Unfortunately, it didn't seem to work too well on a fourteen-year-old boy whose hormones were raging.

"For some reason, my mother doesn't like to talk about my father's death," Leo said first looking at her and then looking around the table.

"Leo, this is not an appropriate conversation to

have at someone else's Thanksgiving table. Stop it. Now." Rebecca tried to be as harsh as possible to get him to stop. It wasn't working.

"I don't get it, Mom. When people ask why we moved here, why can't you just say that is because you couldn't stand to live around all the memories anymore? The memories of how my father died? Why can't you just admit that?" He was staring at her with an almost desperate look on his face that she'd never seen before. It made her want to cry right there in front of everyone.

"Please, Leo, let's just go outside and..." she pleaded as she stood up and pulled on his arm. Everyone else at the table sat there in stunned silence watching the whole thing, and she was sure that they probably never felt more uncomfortable in their lives.

"No! You can never face the truth. Do you realize how difficult you can be sometimes?" he said standing up and slamming his chair into the table before walking out the front door. Rebecca stood there for a moment, tears welling in her eyes, as she scanned the faces of the Parker family.

"I'm... I'm so sorry. This was a mistake. I never should've brought him here. I have to go. I'm sorry..." she said grabbing her purse and her coat before running out the front door after Leo. She didn't have time to be embarrassed right now; although she was sure those feelings would flood her later.

CHAPTER 6

*J*ackson was shocked at what had just happened in front of him. The independent, strong façade of this Rebecca Evans woman was shattered before his very eyes. But he was more shocked at his own feelings. He wanted to protect her, to help her. But he didn't even know her. He wanted to reach out and embrace her and try to calm her down.

And he also wanted to help her son. The punk. The teenager he wanted to slap just yesterday.

He wasn't sure that he had ever seen that level of pain in someone's eyes before today. But the pain wasn't just in Rebecca's eyes. It was in her son's. It was a deep-seated pain that the kid seemed unable to describe with words.

He only knew that he wanted to help both of them, so he grabbed his coat and told everyone he'd be right back. He ran straight out the front door, hoping to catch up with Rebecca before she caught up with Leo. He wanted to find out what had happened to her husband, and what had upset Leo so greatly.

He could see her red curls bouncing in the cool November air as she ran toward the beach.

"Rebecca!" he called out to her. At first she didn't answer, but he didn't relent and she finally stopped for a moment to catch her breath and turned around. She looked desperate.

"I have to find him. I think he ran that way, toward the beach," she said trying to get her breath to cooperate.

Jackson finally caught up with her and put his hands on her shoulders. She seemed to jump a bit, but then she eased up. "He'll be okay. He's a teenager, and they can get a little hormonal at times," he said with a slight smile on his face. Her eyes started to fill with tears again, and she nodded biting her lip.

"He's been through a lot," she said as they started walking again. "I guess a lot of this is my fault. Apparently I haven't handled things the right way."

"Parenting isn't easy, especially when you don't

have a partner to help you with it. I'm sure you've done the best you could."

She looked at him and had a quirk of a smile. "You sure aren't the man I met yesterday."

"Yeah, I was having a rough day. Business deal fell apart, and I guess I had a little more of an attitude than normal. I'd like to apologize for that."

"It's okay. I wasn't exactly in my best frame of mind yesterday either. We'll call it even," she said reaching out her hand to shake his as they walked.

"So tell me something. What is it that you're hiding, Rebecca Evans?" Jackson said. Her eyes got large as she heard his question.

"What do you mean?"

"Well, if you're going to help your son, it sounds like his biggest request is that you be honest. Why don't you start with me? What happened to your husband, Rebecca? What exactly are you running away from?"

"You realize that it's really none of your business, right?" she said, a little bit snippy.

"I do. But it sounds like your son is asking you to trust people again. Maybe I can be someone that you can trust around here."

"But I thought you lived in Atlanta. You don't live around here," she said with a smile.

"Don't change the subject."

"Fine. I'll tell you my story as soon as I find my son. Right now I can't think about anything else."

"Well it's a good thing he's standing right over there then." Jackson pointed across the beach where Leo was standing, throwing seashells into the surf. He turned around and cut his eyes at Rebecca and Jackson before continuing this task. "Why don't we sit down right here for a little while? We know he's safe, but it looks like he might want some time alone."

Rebecca slid down into the sand next to Jackson. Nervously, she started making mounds with her hands, so he nudged her with his shoulder.

"Well?" Jackson said.

"You're a very persistent man, aren't you?" she asked with a sad smile.

"I've been told that before, but it usually works well for me. I just want to help, Rebecca. I'm honestly not just being nosy. That's my brother Brad," he said with a laugh.

She chuckled, and then sighed before looking out into the ocean as if it was going to provide her with the answer she needed.

"Okay, here goes. Our lives changed forever on September 11, 2001." She looked at Jackson, and his eyes widened as he put his hand over his mouth.

"On my God."

"See? That's why I had to leave New York. Everything was a reminder. But not only that; people around me kept saying they were sorry. It's been twelve years, and people are still telling me they're sorry. I know they mean well, but I don't need an extra reminder of the tragedy every single day of my life."

"Understandable. I just wasn't expecting that answer. Was your husband in one of the buildings?" Rebecca nodded.

"Yes. He was an investment banker. We had this amazing life going with our two-year-old son, living right there in the heart of Manhattan. And it all fell to pieces because of the terrible acts of a few people on one day."

"I can't even imagine what it was like to go through that." Jackson didn't really know what to say, and he was afraid to express sorrow after what she just said.

"It's funny the things you remember when you go through a tragedy like that. That morning, I didn't get to tell my husband goodbye. He got up earlier because he had a meeting and he needed to prepare for it. He didn't want to wake me apparently, so he just left me a note. It was just a simple note that said I love you and see you at dinner. I've looked at that note a million times since that day, and every time I try to read through the lines. I try to see if there was another message in that note so I can hang onto it, but there never is. He had no idea that he wouldn't come home for dinner. None of us did. And then I was left with a toddler who was asking for his daddy every day for months. How do you explain that to a two-year-old?" She was staring out into the ocean, her eyes full of tears as Jackson watched Leo sit down just outside of the surf and stare into the ocean too.

"I have no idea how you would explain that to a child so young."

"I don't know if I did it right. He never seemed to totally understand it. And now he's become such an angry kid because he's growing up without a father. And apparently I failed him too."

"Rebecca, you can't say that about yourself. No parent is perfect. He's just a teenage boy who needs some direction now."

"And how do you know so much about kids? I mean you don't even have any of your own."

"Because I helped to raise all of my siblings. My

father died when I was very young, and I became the stand-in father for all of them. That's why stayed in January Cove until I was almost thirty years old. I had to help my mother finish raising them."

"Wow. That explains it then. They all look at you like some authority figure, and I couldn't figure it out," she said with a wry smile.

"Thanks for telling me what happened to your husband. I'm honored that you shared that with me." Their eyes met briefly, and the silence was deafening even with the waves crashing to shore.

"I know it seems silly that I kept it a secret, but I was trying to start over. Give us both a fresh start. I'm not sure why he overreacted that way back there. He's never said anything much about his father before."

"Maybe that's the problem. Maybe he feels like you won't talk about your husband because it's so upsetting. But maybe he needs to talk about it."

"I think you might be in the wrong career field. Maybe you need to be a psychologist," she said nudging him with her shoulder. A bolt of electricity moved through his body when she touched him. She was petite in frame, but he felt immense power coming from her, and he wasn't sure what to do with it.

"Nah, I think I'll stick with real estate. Why don't you go talk to Leo, and I'll give you guys some privacy?" he said standing up. She stood up with him, and brushed off her clothes.

"Thank you. You're not such a jackass after all," she said smiling.

"You thought I was a jackass?"

"Well, that's the only word I can say in polite company." With that, she smiled at him and turned around and started walking towards her son. And Jackson had a really bad feeling that he was about to get caught up in the whirlwind that was Rebecca Evans.

AFTER THE EMBARRASSING episode on Thanksgiving, Rebecca tried to avoid any of the Parker family. She even sent Adele Parker an apology note for ruining her Thanksgiving dinner. Even though she had talked to Leo on the beach that afternoon, it didn't heal any of the rifts between them. Hell, she didn't even really know what the rifts were.

Thankfully, Leo was back at school and she could get back to the business of running her coffee shop to take her mind off her troubles. The truth was she was getting really tired of going to bed alone every night. Twelve years had been long enough, but she didn't know how to get back into the dating scene. She felt like she would compare every man to Tom.

He had been her perfect match. Smart, sexy and successful, and he made her feel safe. Until the day that he was no longer there to make her feel safe. But she was tired of bearing the responsibility of life all by herself. She had no one to lean on, no soft place to fall after a long hard day.

And she had to admit that Jackson Parker would be a worthy dating partner if only he lived in January Cove. And if he was interested in her at all. It had been so long since she had dated anyone that she couldn't tell the signals anymore. Things had changed a lot on the dating scene, and she didn't want to assume that someone was flirting with her or was interested in her if they weren't. She didn't need an embarrassing episode on top of everything else she had going on in her life.

It was early morning, and she started scrubbing the milk nozzle on the cappuccino machine when she heard the doorbell chime as the first customer of the day came in.

"Welcome to Jolt," she said as she turned around. Then she saw him. "Jackson."

"Good morning, Rebecca," he said with a smile. It was certainly a different face than he had the other day when he came into her coffee shop the first time.

"What are you doing here?" There was something about Jackson Parker that did something to her. She felt the nervousness rising from the core of her being, and she wasn't sure why. He was plenty handsome, for sure, but she'd been around handsome men in her life before.

"What am I doing here? In a coffee shop?" He raised his eyebrow at her and smiled.

"Of course. Of course. What can I get for you?" she said nervously trying to figure out what to do with her hands. She finally settled on grabbing a dish towel and wiping up invisible liquid on the counter.

"Just black coffee. No girly drinks today." She smiled and walked away to pour the coffee while Jackson stood at the counter. She could feel his eyes staring at the back of her head, and the little hairs on her neck went up. Why was he looking at her like that?

"Here you go. Anything else?" she asked. He looked at her for a moment and then looked down at his coffee before finally speaking.

"Yeah. Actually, I wanted to ask you a question." Now she was really getting nervous. Was he about to ask her out on a date? She steeled herself, unsure of what her answer would be if he did.

"Okay, ask away," she said feeling a little like a schoolgirl again.

"Does your son like to play football?" Inside, she felt her heart sink. What did she expect him to ask her? And why did she feel so disappointed all of a sudden?

"Um, I think he does. I've seen him throw the football around with his friends back home before. He really doesn't know many people here, though. And his grades aren't good enough to try out for the high school football team this year." She shrugged her shoulders and sighed. Leo's problems seemed to take up every waking moment of her life now. She never would've expected that out of him. He'd been such a good kid and so close to her. They were all each other had for so many years, but now she could feel him pulling away and she didn't know what to do about it.

"Well, then, maybe I can stop by sometime and take him to throw the ball around for a while. I used to play for JCHS when I was his age." Jackson had been a pretty good player at January Cove High School back in his day.

She cocked her head and looked at him confused. "I thought you were going back to Atlanta."

"Well, I might make some changes in my schedule. I haven't taken time off in years, and January Cove has a lot more interesting things going on these days than I thought it would." He slid the money across the counter and picked up his cup of coffee, took a sip and winked. "See you around, Rebecca," he said before walking out the door. Rebecca literally had to fan herself as the door closed behind him. Yep, that Jackson Parker had something going on and she needed to stay as far away from it as possible or risk having her heart broken all over again.

CHAPTER 7

*K*yle Parker was nervous, probably more nervous than he'd ever been in his entire life. He and Jenna had been together most of the time they were growing up, and back together for a few months now. They lived together and raised her daughter together, but the thought of proposing to her was making him sick. He knew it was the right thing to do because he wanted to spend the rest of his life with her, but he wanted to make sure that the proposal was perfect and it was causing anxieties to crop up that he didn't know he had.

"Okay, so do you think that releasing doves would be too much?" he asked Jackson across the table. They had met up for lunch, and Jackson was just

87

digging into his roast beef sandwich when Kyle had broached the subject of planning the engagement.

"Doves?" he said almost choking on his sandwich.

"What's wrong with doves? They're nice-looking birds..." Kyle said throwing his hands up as he looked down at his list he'd made of all the things he wanted to do.

"Don't you think you should leave something for the wedding itself? I mean doves?" Jackson said laughing. "We have a million seagulls flying around out there, and you want to add doves? What if they don't get along? You don't want to be responsible for the great Dove War, do you?"

Kyle shoved Jackson's shoulder across the table causing him to drop half of his sandwich on the floor. Jackson stared at it for a moment as if he couldn't believe what his brother had just done. "I just want to make this as special as possible for her. It's been a rough few years for Jenna." Jackson continued staring at his lost sandwich for a moment before looking back at Kyle.

"Look, man, she just wants to marry you. For whatever reason, the woman is in love with you. I don't think the engagement moment will matter nearly as much as you think it will."

"See? This is why you don't have a woman. The engagement is hugely important to women. That right there shows you just don't understand how women work. I've got to get this thing just right so she has this wonderful memory for the rest of her life. I read it in all of the magazines." Kyle looked down at his paper and Jackson started snickering to himself.

"You've been reading women's magazines? What is wrong with you?" he asked shoving his brother's shoulder across the table in retaliation.

"When you fall in love, for real, you'll understand. I would do anything for Jenna even if it means having to buy women's magazines two counties over," Kyle said starting to laugh himself. "I know I'm going overboard, but I just want to make it special for her."

"Then stop thinking with your head, brother. Think with your heart. You know her better than anyone else on earth. I think you can come up with something that would mean the world to her."

Kyle nodded and closed up his notebook. "So what's going on with you? Anything new on the love front?"

"Of course not. I'm here visiting you losers. I have

to go back to Atlanta to find women," Jackson said with a smile.

"You can't fool me. You might be my older brother, but you've got a terrible poker face. I think you have a little bit of interest in someone right here in January Cove," Kyle said finally taking a bite of his sandwich.

"Oh really? And who would that be?"

"You know who it is. Rebecca Evans. I saw the way you chased her down after her son said that yesterday. I think you've got the hots for her." Kyle took a sip of his sweet tea.

"I do not have the hots for Rebecca Evans. I was simply being nice and trying to help her with a terrible situation. Do you know about her past?" Kyle shook his head.

"I know she moved down here from up north, but that's about it."

"Well, she's a September 11th widow and she's raised Leo by herself. Now he's going through the terrible teens, and he's basically acting out because he didn't have a father figure."

"And you're going to become the father figure?"

"Of course not. I don't even live here. I was just trying to help a woman who was obviously in dire straits yesterday. Any one of us would've done the same, but I run faster." Kyle started laughing.

"Just be careful. Don't get in over your head."

"Okay, Dove Boy. You're giving me advice? I raised four siblings with Mom. I think I can help a woman out with a fourteen-year-old snotty nosed kid."

"I've never seen you quite like this. You normally don't take responsibility for anyone else but yourself. I don't blame you because you spent most of your life raising us, but why this woman?"

"As I said, Kyle, there is nothing going on between me and Rebecca. Strictly a friendship, and a short one at that. I'll be going home soon, and I really won't see her again until Christmas. It's no big deal, so don't go starting rumors."

Kyle could tell Jackson was getting a little bit defensive and uncomfortable, and he knew his brother well enough to know that he should back off.

"So how's business going?" Jackson finally asked after a long, uncomfortable silence.

"Pretty good. I usually buy at least one or two houses every three months. Keeps the bills paid up and allows us to have fun as a family."

"Yeah, my business is booming right now too, but it's a little bit more than I can handle some days."

"Have you ever thought about bringing on a partner?"

"Not really. At least not seriously."

"Let me ask you something, Jackson. What do you want? I mean what do you see in your future? Family? Being eternally single?"

Jackson sat there for a moment seriously considering his brother's question before answering. "I'd like to have a family someday." In a way, he surprised himself. He almost looked around the room to make sure he was the one speaking.

"You've got to set your life up for it now. You've got to start making some tough decisions about your business because no one is going to want to marry a man who's married to his business. You've got to give up some of that control. You built the company, it's a strong company and you need to start trusting other people to help you run it. You need time off. You used to be this really fun loving guy and now you're nothing but a workaholic. There's no room in your life for a woman, and I think that's why you haven't found one."

"Wow. That was deep, Kyle. Maybe you should get your psychology degree."

"Don't get defensive. You know I'm right. Just think about it." Jackson nodded and the brothers continued eating their lunch before parting ways at the front door.

REBECCA STOOD behind the counter of her coffee shop, staring out the plate glass window at the very few people walking down the street in January Cove. She enjoyed the small town life a lot more than she thought she would when she left New York. There were just too many memories there, too many milestones that had been passed. While being around people who knew her and the places that she and her husband had been should've been a comfort, it was too painful. Even twelve years later, seeing their favorite pizza place or walking past the park bench where he proposed was too much for her.

Still, sometimes in the dead of night when she woke up with nightmares, she wondered if she'd made the right decision for her and her son. She pondered over whether leaving home was the best course of action.

Of course, now it was a little too late to worry about that. She'd set up her life here in the small coastal Georgia town. Jolt was doing well enough, and she was starting to develop a following especially on Friday nights when she had live music in the café. She knew that a new start was what they needed, but it didn't make it any easier to leave everything that she knew behind.

It was getting close to closing time, and she had lots of things to do inside of the coffee shop that evening. For one thing, she wanted to get a head start on the painting. The color in the café was a drab beige color that the previous owner had done. But she wanted the place to be a lot more funky and fun, a lot more beachy. So, her plan was to paint it a pale shade of blue and add all kinds of ocean accents around the room. She had been looking at local thrift stores and garage sales for weeks, finding everything from a big wooden fish to hang on the wall to some old netting used on a fishing boat that she would tack up across the ceiling. She wanted the place to feel like the coolest little beach coffee shop anyone had ever seen.

As she walked across the room and closed the front door, she looked up and down the street at all the little businesses. Many of them had closed and reopened even since she'd been there, and it often worried her whether or not her coffee shop would make it in the long run.

She locked the door and turned the sign to closed before heading around the back of the counter. Once she had counted up the money for the evening and balanced out the cash drawer, she lowered the lights and went upstairs to change her clothes.

She threw on the cruddiest clothes she could find and asked Leo if he might want to help her with the painting but he said no, of course. He was busy watching some reality show that was coming on TV that night while he was simultaneously playing some game on his iPhone.

She wished that he wouldn't shut her out like he was doing, but she knew not to push it. Obviously losing his father had been a bigger impact in his life than she even realized. Maybe he was just being a bratty fourteen-year-old boy full of hormones. Either way, she was trying to tread lightly right now.

She walked back downstairs and started popping open the paint can. She decided that she needed some music in the too quiet coffee shop or else she might just go crazy. The sound of silence was not her friend, and it allowed her to think too many things from her past.

The only problem was that her thoughts right

now weren't about her past. Instead, they revolved around Jackson Parker, and she really didn't want to admit that at all. He was a nice guy, as it turned out, but she wasn't looking for love. As much as she was lonely and would love someone to be there to comfort her, she knew her focus had to be on her son right now. And the truth was that no man in his right mind would want to take on a teenage boy who was acting the way Leo was. She was destined to be alone until he was grown, she thought to herself.

She turned on the 80s music channel and started bopping around the coffee shop. Something about dancing to Madonna and Michael Jackson made her happy. Even though she knew the glass windows would allow people to see her dancing, she didn't really care. After all, she was off duty and didn't have anything to prove to anyone. Besides, the lights were turned down low enough that hopefully no one would notice her horrific dance moves. The downtown area was a virtual ghost town the day after Thanksgiving anyway, so she decided to let loose and have fun.

She dragged the ladder from the back storage room and set it up against the far wall. She couldn't help but dance as she heard some of her favorite songs including Thriller. She was dancing around on the ladder and swooshing the paint up against the wall having a good time when she felt someone looking at her through the window.

Oh crap, she thought to herself.

She turned around to find Jackson was standing in the window with a sly smile on his face waving at her. She smiled back and went to step down off the ladder but slipped and fell right on her butt in the open paint container at the foot of the ladder. Jackson looked horrified in the window, especially since he couldn't open the door and help her because it was locked.

She waved her hand at him and said she was okay before she ambled up to her feet, paint dripping down her jeans. This was not the way that she wanted to impress a man. And this is exactly why she didn't date. She was obviously out of practice. Her dance moves might actually have been better than her dating skills, and that thought scared her.

She walked carefully over to the door, dripping paint behind her onto the nice hardwood floors. It made her sick to think of what she was going to have to do with those floors just to make them look nice again.

She opened the door and Jackson immediately

stepped in and grabbed onto her so that she didn't fall down.

"Are you okay? I'm so sorry that I made you fall!" he said pushing the door closed behind them and locking it.

She looked down at the floor with blue paint splattered all over it. "It's not your fault. I had music going and I wasn't paying attention…"

"Come on, let me help you get this cleaned up before it damages the floor."

"I think it's too late. Hardwood floors and paint. I don't think those mix very well," she said shrugging her shoulders and covering her face with her hands. Still, Jackson ran behind the counter and got some wet paper towels and immediately got down on his hands and knees and started wiping up the paint. Luckily, it was coming up fairly easily because it was still so wet. She watched him for a moment, thinking how nice it was that there was a man in her life right now who was willing to help her. Even if he had caused her to divert her attention and fall off the ladder.

"You don't have to do that. I can…" she said trying to reach down and take the paper towels from his hand. He looked up at her, his eyes dark with seriousness, and shook his head.

"Rebecca, you have to let people help you sometimes. Go change your clothes, and I will get this all cleaned up. Okay?" he said. She knew that he wasn't asking a question, but giving her a demand. As she was okay with that. "Oh, and you have a little paint right here..." he said softly as he stood up and reached out, touching her right cheek. She froze in place, her breath seemingly caught in her throat.

"Thanks," she whispered trying not to let him see her trembling. What was he doing to her? He smiled slowly, and lowered his hand. "I'll be right back," she said before backing up.

She went upstairs, and Leo was still watching television and completely paid her no attention. She changed her clothes and washed up before heading back downstairs. Jackson had gotten the floor completely cleaned up and had turned the music down. He was sitting in one of the café chairs when she walked back down the stairs.

"Listen, I'm so sorry that I made you fall. I was just watching you dance, and I was enjoying the show."

"Well, it's not your fault, as I said. And, my dance moves leave a lot to be desired. It's been a long time since I've been out dancing. I only did that during my single days... before I was married."

"I love to dance. In fact, I think I'm one of the only Parker siblings who likes to dance. I'm not sure that I'm good at it, but I like to do it."

She smiled at him for a moment, all too aware that his personality was filling up the space. She felt a little bit like her lungs were deflated, and she couldn't seem to take in a deep breath. What was this guy doing to her? Just the mere thought of him dancing with her had her in knots.

"My husband liked to dance," she said without thinking. She wasn't even sure why she said it, other than to remind herself that she had once had a husband that she loved. That's when it hit her that she was feeling guilt over the fact that Jackson Parker was making her feel things she hadn't felt since she met Tom all those years ago.

"He did? I know a lot of men don't like to dance because they think it's girly. But, I think it's cool if you know how to do it." Jackson seemed undeterred by her mention of her late husband. And why should he feel threatened? Tom was dead. There was no getting around that. Tom wasn't coming back.

Suddenly, Rebecca felt overwhelmed by grief. The kind of grief that she had right after September 11. It was like a distant memory of him dancing had conjured up images that she could barely take.

Suddenly, without any ability to stop it, her eyes welled up with tears and she had to turn around and dab them with a napkin that was lying on the counter.

Jackson got up and slowly walked toward her. Then she felt his strong hands on her shoulders, and his touch made her shiver. She hadn't felt that kind of touch from a man in so long.

"I'm sorry. It's just that sometimes memories flood back and the emotions just grab me."

He slowly turned her around to look at him, but she continued to tilt her head toward the floor. With his finger, he lifted her chin up to make eye contact.

"Rebecca, I can't begin to understand the level of grief that you've gone through. Yes, I lost my father, but that's not the same thing as losing the person that you planned to spend the rest of your life with. It's not the same as being left alone to care for your child for the rest of your life. It's not the same as watching every hope and dream you've ever had go up in smoke, literally. It's not the same as being reminded of his death every time someone mentions that terrible day in September. You've never gotten a real break from any of it. So I can't say that I understand your pain, but I appreciate it. I wouldn't ever want you to stop having memories of your husband.

It sounds like you two had a wonderful love affair, and you shouldn't ever let those thoughts go. But, if I can give you one piece of advice?"

She nodded her head, still unable to speak.

"Don't get so bogged down in the grief that you can't move forward. There's someone else out there for you, someone else who will love you. Not like your husband, but like himself. It will be different, and it should be different. You can't go around comparing every man you meet to your late husband because we are all different. But you deserve to be loved and cared for again. You deserve to have a partner in your life, and you deserve to have someone who will make room for your late husband in the relationship too."

Her eyes widened as she looked up at him. She'd never heard a man speak such beautiful words. And it had never occurred to her that the man that she chose to spend her life with would have to make room for Tom too. He would always be a part of her, if not just in her memories then also in the form of Leo. In that moment, she realized that it was time to move on, and that she could take Tom with her on that journey.

"You okay?" he asked looking at her with his eyebrows furrowed. He still had his hands on her shoulders, and she'd almost forgotten that they were there. It felt so comfortable and comforting that she didn't want him to move them, but he eventually did and shoved them into his pockets.

"I'm fine. It doesn't happen often, but every now and again those memories just come flooding back. It's just not fair. It's not fair what happened to us. It's unfair that some lunatics who wanted vengeance on our country were able to come into it and just take away all those lives. It's not fair that I didn't get to say goodbye and that I loved him. There was no warning. He was just gone. There wasn't even a body to bury. Leo was too young to understand. None of it's fair."

"You're right. I'll never forget where I was and what I was doing on that September day, but it can't compare to what you must be feeling. And whether it's been one year or twelve years or twenty years, you're always going to remember that day. You're always going to wonder what could have been. And I would say that's normal."

"Thank you. I don't normally talk about this with anyone, even my close friend in New York. But it's nice. It's nice to get to talk about it again."

"Any time," he smiled, and again her stomach started doing flip-flops.

"So, what are you doing walking around by yourself on these deserted streets tonight?"

"Well, I was actually coming here to talk to you."

"Talk to me? About what?"

"I was wondering if you and Leo might be interested in taking a little day trip with me tomorrow."

"A day trip? To where?"

"Well, there's a little island that we can get to by boat. Pretty deserted. Not many people go out there, but it's a great place for a picnic and maybe to throw the football around. Would you be interested in joining me?"

"I don't know…"

"Come on. It sounds like you need a little getaway."

"Don't you have to get back to Atlanta?"

"I decided to stay through the weekend. No one's going to be working for the next couple of days anyway, so there's really no reason for me to be back at the office as soon. I think you could both use some time to relax."

She looked down and her face turned red. "Yeah, I'm really sorry about that. I didn't mean to ruin your Thanksgiving. It just goes to show that Leo and I need to spend our Thanksgivings alone so that we don't interfere with other people," she said.

Without warning, he reached over and touched her hand which was resting on the counter. "Rebecca, the last thing you need to be is alone." Their eyes met for a moment, and she could feel electricity ricocheting around inside of her body. She felt like what he was saying to her was a lot more than what it sounded like on the surface. Maybe he was interested after all, but was she interested in him? Was she interested in finally moving forward?

"But what about the coffee shop?"

"Most places on the strip are completely closed for the holiday week, so why don't you just take a day off? Better yet, how about I get Kyle to come over and run the register for you?"

"Do you really think he'd do that?"

"Of course he would. He likes you, and he could drink all the coffee he wanted while you weren't here." Rebecca started laughing.

"In that case, okay. I can't really afford to lose the income, so if Kyle doesn't mind watching the place for a few hours, I'd be totally open to that. Now Leo, on the other hand..."

"Don't worry. You just be ready tomorrow morning around nine o'clock. I'll come by here, and I will convince him that hanging out with us for the day is his best option."

"Well, you must be a magician then."

"Maybe I am."

Without warning, he leaned down and gave her a quick kiss on the cheek before smiling, turning and walking out the door. She was left there stunned, holding her cheek with her right hand. Had Jackson Parker really just kissed her? What on earth was going on in her life?

CHAPTER 8

*J*ackson walked around the side of the building and leaned against the cool brick. What in the world did he just do? He was only here for a short time visiting family for Thanksgiving, but he seemed to be unable to keep away from Rebecca. There was no question that she came with a whole lot of baggage, and he didn't have time for that right now. He had a business to run back in Atlanta and deals that were blowing up, but suddenly he didn't care as much about all that.

"Hey, Jackson. Everything okay?" He looked up and noticed Tessa walking down the sidewalk in front of him.

"Oh. Hi, Tessa. Yeah. I'm fine." He sounded

shaken, and he wasn't even sure why. Maybe it was the fact that he'd just kissed Rebecca Evans on the cheek or that he had promised her he was going to get her son to agree to come to the island with them tomorrow.

"I don't know you very well yet, Jackson, but you sure don't seem fine. You look like you just saw a ghost." She was offering him a sweet smile and touching his shoulder.

"Actually, I am a little more anxious this morning than normal." He smiled and put his hands in his pockets.

"Does this have anything to do with Rebecca Evans?" She asked crossing her arms and jutting her hip out. How did women always know stuff like that? It was like they were mind readers. Maybe men just weren't as complicated as they hoped they were.

"Why would you say that?" he asked trying to keep a smile off his face.

"Because I saw how you acted around her on Thanksgiving. She put you on edge, for sure. I consider myself to be a pretty good judge of character, and I think you have the hots for Rebecca Evans." She wagged her finger at him and laughed.

"I'm not sure if I like *you* anymore."

"That's okay. You'll learn to love me. How about

we go take a walk on the pier and chat? I might be able to help you." He thought about it for a moment. Did he really want to take a walk and chat about Rebecca? For some strange reason, he did.

They walked across the street to the beginning of the pier. It was a beautiful day, clear blue skies and a nice breeze. It wasn't so cold that it was uncomfortable, which was one of the perks of living near the beach.

"So, tell me what's going on this morning that has you so frazzled," Tessa said, getting right down to business.

"Where do I begin? I'm sure my brothers told you that I'm not someone who settles down easily with women." He cut his eyes over at her, but she had a pretty good poker face it seemed.

"I've heard some stories. But I think that's just a protection mechanism." There she goes, reading my mind again, he thought.

"Protection mechanism?" He acted as if he had no idea what she was talking about, but in reality she nailed it. Bull's-eye.

"Yeah. You were the leader of your family for your whole life. You were in charge as the man of the family after your father passed away. All of that responsibility so young probably made you want to run off as soon as you could to start your life. But it also made you wary of getting too close to someone who might leave you."

"Ah, sounds like we might have a new psychologist in the family," he said trying to hide his nervousness.

"Come on, Jackson. Be serious. I know it must've been hard to have so much responsibility as a young kid. And then on top of that, you go off to find yourself and create a career, but you can't connect with a woman. You're afraid of being alone, but at the same time you're afraid of falling in love and risking your heart."

Jackson looked over at her, and he could see a hint of sadness in her eyes. He knew Tessa's story. Abused by her husband, ran away to save herself and her son. When Aaron had gotten involved with her just a few short weeks ago, he'd worried about his brother getting involved with someone who had so much baggage. And when her abusive husband was killed right there in Aaron's RV park, he wasn't sure if the two of them would stay together. But she loved his brother, and she'd been through worse than anything Jackson could've imagined.

"You're probably right, but it's hard to change at my age."

"It's hard to change at any age, Jackson. The question is, how much do you want it? How much do you want to be in love and have a stable woman beside you? And how much are you willing to risk?" All were good questions, but he didn't have any answers.

"Things to think about, I guess," he said shooting a look at her.

"So tell me what's going on today. Did you ask her on a date or something?"

"Sort of. I guess…"

"Well, I hope you're more sure of yourself when you're talking to Rebecca," she said with a laugh as she bumped his shoulder with her own.

"Me too. I invited her and her son over to this little island that I know about tomorrow morning. Thought we might have a picnic."

"Her son? Do you think you can handle that?"

"I helped raise four siblings, so I can handle a punk fourteen-year-old kid."

"My first piece of advice would be not to talk about her son like that. You might slip up, and a mother doesn't want to hear you refer to her son as a punk."

"Good advice. I should stop saying that. The kid has obviously been through a lot, losing his father the way he did."

"I imagine he's been through more than we can even fathom. You have a lot in common with him, losing your dads at a young age."

"We do, but at least I got to know my father during my early years of life. Leo doesn't remember his father, and I think he's angry. And I bet he doesn't even know why he's angry. He's missing something he doesn't even understand, and it's becoming more important during these formative years. He has no man to show him how to be a man."

"Sounds to me like you want to be there for this kid and his mother."

"I don't know what I want. I just have to take it day by day. I mean, I don't even live in January Cove. My life and my business are in Atlanta, so I probably shouldn't be pursuing this at all right now."

"The thing is, you can't always do what your head is telling you. Sometimes, you have to let your heart be in control." He knew she was speaking from experience.

They reached the end of the pier and sat down, their legs dangling over the ocean. Jackson always found peace at the ocean. Something about those waves coming in and out, always bringing something new to the shore every moment of every day.

It reminded him that life can change on a dime, in good ways and bad ways.

"I know you're right."

"So why did you invite Rebecca and her son on a day trip?"

"I guess I just felt sorry for her. I know she's struggling trying to get him in line, and I remember what that was like to lose my father. I really want to help both of them, but I feel a little bit powerless to tell you the truth. I mean, I've got an entire life back in Atlanta that I need to go home and tend to, but something is keeping me here. And this time it's not my own family."

Tessa looked over at him and smiled. "Jackson, I think you're kidding yourself. You don't want to stay here because you feel sorry for her. You want to stay here because you feel sorry for you."

He looked at her for a moment, unsure of what she meant. "Excuse me?"

"Please, don't take offense to what I just said. But I think the real reason that you invited Rebecca and her son on a day trip, and the real reason you're not going back to Atlanta immediately, is because you know that you've been missing out on love. You've spent your whole life taking care of other people, so I fail to believe that this is just another charity case you're taking on. From what your brothers have told me, you are a pretty ruthless businessman back in Atlanta. You could easily be back there right now, but you're not. I think you're sticking around because you see something in Rebecca. You see some kind of potential, and your brain and your heart are having a disagreement. Now you just have to decide which one is going to win the argument."

"And how does that indicate that I feel sorry for myself?"

"Because you finally know that there might be someone out there for you, and you're feeling conflicted and almost victimized by your circumstances. A job and a life in Atlanta are circumstances of your own making, Jackson. You set that life up, and you have the power to change your life. One decision can do that. For me, the decision to head South changed my life when I ran out of gas in January Cove. For you, the decision to go on a picnic might just change your life if you let it."

With that, Tessa stood up and brushed down the sides of her long skirt. Jackson looked up at her, shielding his eyes from the bright sunlight.

"Where are you going?" he asked.

"I've got some shopping to do, and then I'm meeting your brother for lunch. Plus, I think you need a little time alone to figure out what you're going to do next. I hope you make the right decision." She reached down and squeezed his shoulder before turning and walking back up the pier. He watched her for a moment, and listened to the clicking of her boots as she walked out of sight. In that moment, he was able to clearly see what his brother, Aaron, saw in her. She was sassy, honest to a fault and beautiful to boot. And he hoped that someday he would find a woman who would challenge him in that same way. And then it occurred to him that maybe he already had.

REBECCA WAS NERVOUS, more nervous than she'd been in quite some time. Maybe it was the fact that she hadn't broken the news to her son yet that they were going on this day trip with Jackson Parker. Maybe it was the fact that she hadn't been around many men like him in a long time. This felt an awful lot like a date even though her son would be there, and she didn't know what to make of that.

Leo would be home any minute now, and she wasn't sure how to broach the subject of the day trip. He'd gone out skateboarding with a friend of his from school, and she had to admit that she welcomed peace and quiet for a few hours. She loved her son, but being fourteen and fatherless seemed to have done things to his personality that she was incapable of undoing.

As she took her last sip of coffee, she heard him keying the lock to the door of their small apartment above the coffee shop. She had closed down early, mainly due to lack of traffic and her inability to concentrate after Jackson's visit. If she'd had any customers, she would've stayed open just because they needed the money. But it was a virtual ghost town in January Cove anyway, and staying open was just useless.

"Hey, honey. Did you have a good time?" she asked as he walked in and slid into one of the chairs beside the sofa. She hated how his hair hung in his eyes now, but that was the popular look apparently. Seemed like every boy she saw in his age range had hair longer than she did when she was a kid.

"Yeah. We went down by that old abandoned shopping center at the edge of town."

"What? I didn't give you permission to go all the way to the edge of town. You said you were going to the school parking lot."

"We changed our minds. There were too many

cars still in the parking lot. I guess some of the teachers left their cars there over the holiday weekend." He flipped the hair out of his eyes and started texting on his phone. Sometimes, she really hated the advancements in technology. It seemed like electronics were putting a wedge between her and her son.

"Next time, at least give me a call to let me know where you are."

"Fine." He sighed and reached across the table to take a handful of candy corn that was still left in a dish from Halloween.

"Listen, don't make any plans for tomorrow. We're going on a day trip." She steeled herself for what was to come because Leo liked to argue about everything anyway. As soon as he found out they were going with Jackson, she was sure that he was going to blow a gasket.

"A day trip? To where?"

"To a little island that we can get to by boat. We're going to have a picnic and maybe throw the football around." She tried not to make eye contact as she wiped down one of the kitchen counters.

"You're going to throw the football around with me?" He laughed, and for just a moment she wished she had a ball to hurl at his head. But then she remembered that she couldn't throw a football to save her life and would likely just end up breaking her favorite vase.

"No," she said as she continued straightening up the kitchen without looking at him, "Jackson Parker is taking us." A deafening silence fell over the room. She didn't turn around, but instead waited for him to say something. But he didn't. It was just quiet. "Did you hear me?" she asked as she turned around and looked at him. He had put his phone on the table and was crossing his arms and leaning back in his chair glaring at her.

"Yeah, I heard you all right. And if you think I'm going with that jerk to an island, you've lost your mind." He started to stand up, but she walked in his path. He was taller than her now, and sometimes it made her concerned that if his anger ever got the best of him they might end up in a physical confrontation. She'd never known him to be that way, but as a single mother of a hormonal teenage boy, she didn't know what to expect. He didn't know his own strength, and it was times like these that she missed having a male figure in the household.

"Now, you just wait a minute, Leo. You would do well to remember that I am your mother. I am the parent here. You don't get to make decisions for yourself until you're eighteen years old and out of my house. So if I say we're going on a day trip with a friend of mine, that's exactly what we're doing." He stared down at her as if he was shocked by her tone before she stepped out of the way and walked back into the kitchen without a word. She was hoping a little tough love might shock his system. A few moments later, she heard him shut his bedroom door quietly. She had no idea what that meant, but at least it didn't produce a huge argument. She could only hope that he would behave himself when Jackson showed up the next morning to take them on the boat. And she could only hope that she knew how to behave around Jackson herself.

CHAPTER 9

*E*arly morning at the beach had always been one of Jackson's favorite times of the day. But today he just found himself a bundle of nerves. As he rounded the corner in his car to pull up in front of Jolt, he could swear that his hands were sweating for the first time in his adult life. He did multi-million dollar real estate deals, yet a certain red head was making him sweat?

Why did Rebecca make him so incredibly nervous? Or maybe it was that he knew that her son was going to give him problems as soon as he walked in the door. Or maybe a miracle happened and the boy would be excited to go. Yeah, right.

He parked his car in front of the coffee shop in one of the few spaces on the square of January Cove. Looking around his car one more time to make sure that it was tidy enough for guests, he locked the door with the remote and approached the glass door to the coffee shop. As he walked inside, his brother, Kyle, greeted him with a big grin from behind the counter.

"Welcome to Jolt," he said with a beaming smile. Jackson just shook his head and laughed at his brother.

"I guess if that whole real estate investment business doesn't work out, you can always pour coffee for a living."

"You laugh, but I've poured several cups this morning without spilling a drop."

"So, where's Rebecca?"

"She's upstairs finishing up her makeup, from what I understand. I haven't seen Leo this morning, but I assume he's going with you?"

"I hope so. I guess she talked to him about it last night, but I don't know what his reaction was."

Just then, Jackson could hear someone walking down the steps from their apartment. He saw her legs before he saw her. She was wearing a long beige colored flowing skirt and a pair of cowboy boots. And she looked good. Very good, in fact. He thought for a moment how the women back in the big-city didn't look like Rebecca Evans. They looked over-made, but she had a kind of rare, natural beauty that he'd never seen before.

"Good morning," she said, and he was pretty sure she was blushing already. Redheads tended to do that.

"Good morning," Jackson said hoping he wasn't blushing too. "Where's Leo?"

Before she could answer, he heard footsteps coming down the stairs. "Relax. I'm coming. I've been informed that I can't make decisions until I'm eighteen." Jackson wanted to laugh at that remark when he saw Rebecca trying to keep from smiling herself. Apparently she had laid down the law with her son before he had the chance to.

"Well, good. I'm glad you're joining us, Leo. I brought the football…"

"Look, dude, I'm not ten years old. I don't need you to throw the football with me or teach me how to fish or show me how to be a man. If you're thinking I'm some kind of charity case that you need to fix, don't bother."

"Leo!" Rebecca said pointing her finger at him.

"No, it's okay Rebecca. I understand where he's coming from. I lost my dad young, and I would've reacted the same to any man who came around me then too. But, Leo, I was only bringing the football because your mom said you might want to try out for the team at the high school next year. I thought maybe we could throw it a bit and see if you have any skills." Again, Rebecca tried not to giggle.

"Who made you the football king?" Leo said crossing his arms and jutting his chin out like he was challenging Jackson.

"No one, I guess. It's just I was an All-Star all four years in high school, and I know the coaches personally. In fact, I played with all of them in high school." With that, Jackson waved at Rebecca and started toward the door.

"Well maybe we can throw it around a little bit," Leo said moving a little more quickly than Jackson would have imagined. Maybe he had a chance with this boy after all.

REBECCA HAD to admit that she was impressed with the way Jackson had nonchalantly handled her son. She had never seen Leo change his tune so quickly,

RACHEL HANNA

but she was happy to see that Jackson wasn't scared to stand up to him. If she was honest with herself, it was kind of nice to have a strong man standing behind her for once, even if it was just for the day.

She had no illusions that this was anything but a nice guy trying to help a woman who was obviously in distress with her son. But she needed some time away from the coffee shop, and she needed some new people to support her in January Cove. Now that her secret was out, there was really no need to keep hiding out in her tiny apartment over Jolt.

"After you," Jackson said, opening the passenger door for her.

"Thank you," she said with a smile as she tucked her long skirt under her and slid into the seat. Leo opened the back door and flopped down in the seat just behind hers.

Once Jackson was behind the wheel, he shot her a glance and a smile. Her stomach knotted up in a way it hadn't since she'd met her husband all those years ago. Even when she was dating for that brief moment in time a few years back, she hadn't had those feelings. But there was something about this Jackson Parker guy.

"So, have you been on the ferry yet?" he asked as he pulled onto the main road.

"No. I didn't even know there was a ferry until you mentioned it," she said with a laugh. She hadn't spent a lot of time sight seeing since moving to January Cove. Her focus had been only on her business and her son, both of which took up plenty of her time.

"Well, you're going to love the island. It doesn't even officially have a name, but the boat captain knows me from high school so he takes the occasional side trip and drops me off there."

"I guess it pays to have connections," she said raising her eyebrows. "You take a lot of dates over there?" Oh, goodness, why would she ask a thing like that?

"No. I live in Atlanta. Remember?" he said cocking his eyebrow up at her.

"Oh. Right."

"Seriously, though, I've only gone to the island with family and a couple of buddies from high school back in the old days. It's a special place to me."

"Well, we can't wait to see it. Right, Leo?" she said turning slightly. Leo was slouched in his seat, looking out the window as the small town passed before his eyes. He didn't respond or look at her, but she didn't want to start an argument so she left it alone.

A few minutes later, they pulled into the parking lot where the ferry left. Jackson opened his door and immediately came around to open hers. Southern chivalry was something she was really starting to love. Leo opened his own door and stood beside the car, hands in his jean pockets.

"Jackson Parker! Holy hell, man, how long's it been?" a man said walking toward Jackson from the dock.

"Clay! Man, you got fat!" Jackson yelled back laughing at his obvious attempt at humor since the man was muscular and cut like a bodybuilder.

They did the requisite "man hug" and then pushed each other like two twelve year old boys.

"Rebecca Evans, this is one of my oldest friends in the world, Clay Hampton," Jackson said smiling as he put one arm around his friend.

"Nice to meet you, Rebecca. I'm sorry you had to ride with this city boy," he said laughing.

"Whatever. And this is her son, Leo," Jackson said as he cocked an eye at Clay. It was apparent to Rebecca that Jackson had said something to Clay about her son's attitude. She hated that Leo was getting such a bad reputation in their small town already.

"Hey, Leo. Nice to meet you," Clay said extending his hand. Leo didn't look up or take his hand. Instead, he mumbled a halfhearted "hey" and then sighed as he walked toward the dock.

"I'm sorry," Rebecca said with a weary smile. "He's been having some issues lately..."

"Listen, you don't have to explain. Really. I totally understand. I remember how this guy acted after his father died," he said pointing at Jackson. "He'll get through this. Just part of being a hormonal teenager."

Rebecca was thankful for such a kind person. Everyone seemed kind in January Cove. It was like an oasis in the middle of a world filled with anger and danger. She wondered what Clay's story was, because she could definitely tell that he had one, but she decided to leave that for another day.

Jackson retrieved some items from his trunk as Clay motioned for them to come to the ferry. They all passed Leo, but he eventually followed. The ferry wasn't huge, but it had an upper deck which was where Jackson led them. Clay took control of the vessel, and a few moments later they were pulling away from the dock.

"Are we the only ones on here?" Rebecca asked incredulously as they pulled away.

"Yep. He normally wouldn't be doing a run today, but it pays to know people," Jackson said laughing.

Leo sat down on one of the bench seats and leaned over, watching the water as they started the journey to the island.

"Wanna sit?" Jackson asked, yelling a little over the roaring of the engine as it started to cut through the water.

"Sure," she said, almost a little nervous to be somewhat alone with him. He motioned for them to take a seat on another bench seat across the ferry from Leo.

"He'll be fine, Rebecca," he said as he waved her over. She smiled and sat down, still looking at her son.

"I'm so tired of worrying about him," she said, which was possibly the most honest thing she'd said in years. She was tired. Exhausted was more like it. She was tired of being alone, shouldering the weight of every worry life threw at her all on her own. She wanted some big, broad shoulders to carry the weight with her, but her son had to come first.

"You know, I remember after my father died, I once caught my mother on her knees in her bedroom crying. I didn't really understand what was happening. Here I was, grieving the loss of my Dad, and now my mother appeared to be falling apart too. I just stood there, frozen in place. My mother looked over at me. I could see her face totally change," he said, staring out into the water. "A minute later, her tears were dried, she was on her feet and she was asking me what I wanted for dinner. She just stood up and walked past me like nothing ever happened. That's when I realized that mothers are different."

"What do you mean?" Rebecca asked softly as his eyes met hers.

"I mean that mothers have some innate ability to just keep going even when times get really bad. They just move forward, carrying the weight of their family on their shoulders when needed. I really respect that."

His words took her breath away for a moment. No one had ever really captured what she had been feeling all these years in words, but he did. How was that even possible? No one could really know the pain of losing a spouse in such a public way. And then having to raise a son who seemed intent on being miserable.

"Thanks," was all she could manage to say for a moment.

"Listen, Rebecca, I know you're worried about Leo but he's going to be okay. I'm living proof of that." He had no idea how much his words meant to her. As he looked at her with those smoldering eyes, it took everything in her not to grab him and press her lips to his. She wanted to get lost in him, but she knew that would be a big mistake because he didn't live in January Cove. She had to focus her energy on her new business and her son. That was all she could handle right now. "You still with me?" Jackson asked, breaking her train of thought. She realized he had put his hand over hers in an effort to comfort her, but suddenly it felt like her skin was on fire. She quickly slid her hand up and pointed into the water.

"Is that a fish?" was all she could think to say. She wanted to literally put her foot in her mouth.

"Rebecca, are you okay?" he asked with a chuckle.

"I'm fine. Of course. Why?" she said, sure that he could see her hands literally shaking. What on Earth was wrong with her? She felt like a school girl again.

"I didn't mean anything by touching your hand," he said softly in her ear. His breath was warm and inviting on her cheek.

"I know. I'm sorry. I don't know what's wrong with me this morning," she said. He smiled at her, and her heart melted. He knew. He absolutely knew that she was attracted to him. Just great.

"There's the island," he said pointing off in the distance.

"Oh wow, that was quick. It's beautiful. Do you think anyone else is there?"

"Nope. Just us," he said with a sly smile. "Come on, let's go." Jackson stood up and reached a hand down to her. She took his and immediately let go once she was standing. She was almost sure she heard him chuckle under his breath, but she couldn't be positive.

They walked over to Leo and alerted him that the island was coming up quickly. Clay pulled up to the small docking area a few moments later. Jackson explained that he and his brothers had helped to build the dock area when they were kids just so the ferry could take people to the island. Most of the locals knew about the island but didn't go there often, so Jackson considered it an oasis. It was the one place on Earth that never changed. Never became crowded like the city.

"One more thing," Jackson said to her before they departed the ferry.

"What?" she asked. He pulled her arm to get her further from Leo.

"Let me work with him today, okay?" She looked at him questioningly. "Trust me." His eyebrows raised up, and she knew he was serious.

As they stepped off the ferry, Rebecca looked around, pleasantly surprised that no one else was on the island yet nervous at the same time. She watched as Jackson scouted ahead and found a spot to set up the picnic wondering what in the world she'd gotten herself into. Although, nerves were a small price to pay if he was able to help her with Leo.

Jackson set out the blanket and basket on a small patch of grass just above the sand. The whole island seemed to be on a small mound with grass near the top and sand around most of the bottom. Large waves crashed behind them and mixed with the sounds of seagulls. It sure didn't feel like she was in Georgia anymore.

Rebecca took Jackson's goofy grin as a signal that she was supposed to come sit down. She looked around for Leo and noticed that he was already up to no good, poking at what looked like a dead jellyfish washed ashore with a stick. She shook her head and called to him "Leo, why don't you come and eat?"

Without even looking up, he replied "I'm not hungry." Rebecca wasn't in the mood for this right now, so she decided to just go sit on the blanket with Jackson and let him deal with it however he planned to.

As she lowered herself onto the blanket, she noticed that among the man items set out by Jackson for their picnic was a bottle of wine. This was beginning to feel more and more like a date by the moment. The thought sent goosebumps running up her spine as she felt his eyes on her. "So what do you think of the island?" Jackson's voice startled Rebecca out of her thoughts, and she looked up at him to see how the loose tendrils of his black hair were blowing around in the sea breeze.

"It's a very peaceful place, Jackson. I can see why you and your family might like it." She looked back down at all the food in front of them and questioned, "So, what's for lunch?"

"Well, nothing but the finest leftovers in the history of leftovers. We've got turkey sandwiches, mashed potatoes and stuffing." Jackson made her giggle, and she could feel herself blush. She was so embarrassed acting like a little girl with an almost grown son. For a moment they looked at each other, and she felt his fingers creep just close enough to touch the tips of hers. She was suddenly entranced looking at this handsome businessman who had kissed her on the cheek and offered to help her tame her son. How crazy she was to be having these silly schoolgirl moments with a man she just met that would probably be back in Atlanta in a few days time.

The trance was broken when Leo appeared, a shadow standing above Rebecca. "Okay, now I'm hungry." Jackson chuckled under his breath a little, and Rebecca tried to keep the smile off her face as Leo grabbed a sandwich and sat down next to Jackson, peeking at the football behind Jackson's back.

They all took his cue and began to eat as he practically scarfed down his sandwich. Rebecca wondered if this is what it would be like if they still had a full family; picnics on the beach and a quiet that gave her peace. For the first time in twelve years, she didn't feel a gaping hole in her heart. She felt... at ease. Calm. Peaceful. It made her think about the things Jackson had said about having to find a man that would accept the fact that her husband would always be a part of her life. Was Jackson referring to himself? She hated to read too much into signals she couldn't be sure were there after all these years of not dating, but she had come to January Cove to start over. Maybe this was part of it.

Jackson poured a glass of wine for both of them

and tossed soda over to Leo. Leo caught it one handed. "You have a good arm, kid. I can't wait to see what you can do with a pig skin."

"A pig skin?" Leo looked up at his mother, his mouth full of turkey and mayonnaise. Rebecca was about to say something about manners but decided against it.

"That's another term for football. It's made of pig's skin. It's a Southern thing." She watched him shake his head as she and Jackson both chuckled. Rebecca remembered living up North how people would talk about Southerners. They did seem to have a language all their own, but their slower paced lifestyles made her feel more at ease than the bustling of businesspeople in New York.

Rebecca sipped at her wine and noticed Jackson guzzling his. She hadn't noticed before, but he was clearly a little tense. After probably his third glass of wine he got up and grabbed the football. "You ready, Leo?"

"Hang on. I want to see if I have a text first."

"Oh c'mon, man. Football's much more interesting than a text." That's when Jackson let the ball fly straight at Leo, and Leo barely caught it, the ball thumping into his stomach with an ooph noise.

"Bring it on, old man!" Delighted at her son's

response, Rebecca turned to watch her son chase after Jackson and throw the ball toward him then running after him trying to tackle him. Maybe a man is what he had needed all along, and Rebecca just hadn't seen it because she'd been too worried to try and replace a husband and a father that couldn't be.

CHAPTER 10

Jackson was happy that the football idea was working, but he was surprised by how out of shape he'd become. Really, he shouldn't be surprised since high school was quite a long time ago. All he ever did these days was stay holed up in his office making business deals, but it just made him feel that much older. He didn't like that.

It made him not only think about the fact that he was old and unmarried but also about all the things he'd been missing while just sitting in his office. He'd missed his family as well as many hobbies that he should've kept this whole time. Instead he'd been worried about money and work. Maybe it was about time for a change of pace.

He called out as the football hit him in the side of the head, nicking his ear. "Heads up, old man!" Leo called to him, half joking, half annoyed.

Jackson chuckled. "Hey, when you're this old, you'll understand. Maybe we should take it down a notch for a few and just throw the ball. Maybe you can help me get back in shape."

"I thought you were like some big football guy or something."

Jackson threw the ball back at Leo. "That's right. I was. Unfortunately, that was farther in the past than I'd like to admit." For the first time since meeting Leo, Jackson saw him smile a little.

"I knew you were just trying to impress my mom."

Jackson wasn't sure why, but he almost took offense to that statement, but he held his anger back. "What makes you say that?"

"Oh, c'mon. It's so obvious you like my mom. What's even worse is that she likes you too, but you both are being all shy and shit. I mean the guy's been six feet under for years now. You can't hurt a pile of ash."

Jackson caught the ball and stopped for a moment. There was that anger again, creeping up on this boy from a place inside he didn't even know existed. "First of all, I'm pretty sure your mother wouldn't want you to use that kind of language. I get that it sounds cool right now, but really it just sounds unintelligent." Jackson watched Leo cross his arms and try to shut himself off. "Look, your mother loved your father a lot, more than either of us understand since we haven't ever felt that way about someone before. You weren't old enough to know him when he passed, and he was stolen from you. I can see how all of it can seem confusing and make you angry. You feel a hole for something you don't understand because you never had it in the first place. Did you know my father died?"

Leo uncrossed his arms and shook his head. "No. I didn't. What happened to him?"

"He was in a car crash, and my mother was devastated. The thing is, she never let us see how much it hurt her because she knew we all hurt too, and we needed her to be strong for us. My siblings were lucky. I was old enough to step up and help out, but you didn't have that. Your mother is trying to be two parents to you, and it's an impossible thing to do. So, could you do me a favor, and cut her some slack? She's hurt already from losing her husband, she would be heart broken to lose you too."

Leo stopped for a moment and ran his fingers

through his hair. For the first time, Jackson thought he might have seen a chink in the boy's armor. "I know. I just sometimes feel like everyone knows more about my father than me. It just isn't fair. Now my mom takes me across the country, and now I know even less about him. No one knows him here. I know how that might be better for her, and I don't know why I'm so angry. I just wish I had someone who understood more things about me. Like, my mom's only half. She doesn't really date, either, so I don't really have any guy to talk to at all. There was one guy once, but it didn't last very long. And this might shock you, but I think you'd be good for her, Jackson, but not if you're just gonna run off. So, please, don't get in too deep if that's what you're gonna do."

"I thought you didn't like me," Jackson said with a rueful smile.

"That's up to you," Leo responded, not smiling at all.

Jackson felt a weight on his shoulders just then, and decided to throw the football to Leo again. He nodded to acknowledge that he understood what Leo was saying. Clearly, he had some things to think about, but here on the beach with this beautiful woman and her child probably wasn't the place to do it.

All of a sudden they both heard laughing in the distance and realized they were no longer alone on the island. They both headed toward the sound to find Rebecca standing with Kyle and Jenna. He could see that Jenna was wiping her eyes, and Kyle was beaming. Jackson had a feeling that he'd missed something big.

Kyle ran up to him, breaching the distance between them and grabbed him in a bear hug. Jackson realized that his elation must've meant he'd proposed to Jenna and she'd said yes. Jackson hugged Kyle back as Kyle sniffled, clearly trying to keep from tearing up. "She said yes, brother!"

"That's so great, Kyle. Congratulations!" Jackson meant every word of it. He was so happy for his brother, but he couldn't help but feel a pang in his chest as he thought about the fact that he didn't even technically have a girlfriend. It made him feel instantly lonelier, and his eyes glanced over to Rebecca for a moment wondering whether or not he should try and move things along with her.

"Oh, I'm sorry, buddy. We didn't mean to interrupt your date. Is this your first date? It's just that I couldn't stand the nerves and the planning anymore so I brought her to the island and just did it. I had to pay Clay fifty bucks to get him to turn around and come back, but I thought that it was as special as I could get, you know. But hey, you brought Rebecca here on your first date, so she must be pretty important." Kyle winked at Jackson.

Jackson shook his head and was about to protest about being on a date, but who was he trying to fool? He was lecturing this woman's son, he couldn't stop thinking about being alone with her, and he'd brought wine to an island picnic. "Nah, don't worry about it. I wouldn't miss my little brother getting engaged for the world." Jackson put Kyle in a headlock and gave him a quick noogie as they made their way over to the girls.

Jackson got a glimpse of the shine of the ring on Jenna's left hand and the smile on Rebecca's face while looking at it. It sent a shiver down his spine as he imagined a similar scene between him and Rebecca. He felt like he needed to hit his head on a wall because he obviously wasn't thinking clearly.

He walked up to Jenna and gave her a hug. "I'm so glad you finally get to be an official part of the family, Jenna. It's been a long time coming." Jenna smiled warmly, clearly elated and caught up in the moment. He could see streaks on her face where she'd been crying.

"Oh, thanks Jackson. I feel the same way. I just love all of you so much." She fanned herself, about to break down again. Kyle put his arm around her, and he could see that Leo and Rebecca were packing up the picnic basket. These two love birds needed some time to revel in their new engagement.

"Well, we're going to leave you two to it. Enjoy this moment. It's once in a lifetime right?" As Jackson said that, Rebecca appeared at his side, smiling, but he noticed how it didn't quite reach her eyes. He figured that she was probably remembering when her husband proposed to her. He couldn't imagine experiencing a moment like that only to lose the person. No wonder she and her son had some problems. Not that he didn't have problems of his own.

"Oh, we will. By the way, Rebecca, Tessa volunteered to watch the shop for a bit. I'm sorry, but I just couldn't wait any longer to do this. Today just felt right, you know?" Kyle said apologetically.

"No need to apologize, Kyle. I'm sure Tessa is great at making coffee. Congratulations to the both of you." Jackson took a deep breath and grabbed Rebecca's free hand, prompting the other three in their company to raise their eyebrows at him. He ignored it and tried his best not to sweat bullets all over her palm as he led her back to the ferry, which was already waiting since Kyle had obviously brought it over with Jenna.

REBECCA LOOKED DOWN at her hand entwined with Jackson's. It was weird because she saw it but couldn't really feel it because she was so nervous. However, she decided not to let go this time as they climbed onto the ferry and sat down next to each other.

She looked around for Leo and saw that he was already engrossed in his cell phone. She sighed, realizing some battles couldn't be won, but at least he had been willing to throw the ball around with Jackson without too much of a fuss. It made her wonder what they had talked about.

The ride back to the main land was very quiet for the both of them. She couldn't tell if it was from nerves or to avoid ruining the moment. It was at least a welcome distraction from the thoughts that had been going through her head when she saw that Kyle had proposed. It made her remember her own engagement with her husband, and it made her chest ache a little to think about it.

On the other hand it also made her think about the fact that she really hadn't dated a whole lot since his death, and she couldn't imagine as much as he'd loved her that he'd want her miserable and alone forever. Plus, a man would be good in both their lives. Maybe it was time to seize the moment with this Jackson Parker, lest something great passed her by for good.

After the ferry pulled in, she let Leo get ahead of them and climb out before she turned to Jackson and planted a kiss right on his lips. At first he seemed surprised, but then he relaxed into it, opening his mouth slightly. His breath smelled like wine, and though his lips were chapped, they were appealing and strong. She found herself getting lost for a moment not having been able to feel like this for so long. Shocked at herself, she still wasn't able to pull away quickly.

The faraway sound of her son making a retching noise brought her back to reality and made her blush. She was embarrassed, but as she looked into Jackson's eyes, she realized he was just as attracted to her as she was to him. At least she hadn't crossed her signals.

She smiled at him but let her hand slip out of his to catch up with her son. Clearly there was some damage control to be done. She caught up to him and put her arm around him. "Hey, kiddo."

Leo stopped walking for a moment and looked up at her. "Mom, please tell me we aren't about to have the birds and bees talk or something." Taken aback a little, Rebecca laughed.

"Yeah, I guess it would be a little late in life for that one, Leo. I just wanted to say sorry that you had to see that. I know it's not really cool to watch your mom kiss some stranger."

Leo stopped her. "Mom, I get it. You like him, he likes you. It's fine. If you need to have a date or something, I can go play video games at home or at a friend's house. Just don't get all mushy in front of me now, okay?" Surprised by his words, Rebecca hugged him.

She all of a sudden felt a weight lift off her shoulders, and she felt the freedom to feel something for someone again, particularly this successful business man with perfect black hair and a strong football arm.

CHAPTER 11

They reached Jolt sooner than Jackson anticipated, and he couldn't help but feel bummed that the date that he had just realized actually was a date, was about to be over with. He hadn't gotten any true alone time with Rebecca.

He watched her as she walked inside of her coffee shop, and they both were shocked to see how busy it was. Tessa seemed to be handling the influx of customers with pizazz, but Rebecca looked a little embarrassed. She rushed to get behind the counter and help Tessa out. Left standing there alone, Leo walked up to Jackson and held out his hand to shake.

Temporarily taken aback by Leo's almost complete turn around in attitude, it took Jackson a minute to grab his hand to shake. He was even more surprised when Leo, with quite a bit of strength for a boy his age, yanked Jackson's arm so that he could whisper in his ear. "Come back at closing, Jackson. I'll convince her that I can find something else to do." Then, Leo winked and walked away.

Jackson waved at Tessa and Rebecca, but they were both too busy to notice and made his way out of Jolt. He decided to go spend some time with his family and think about what he really wanted in his life.

REBECCA WAS SWEATING when her shift was over, and Tessa noticed it.

"Rebecca, why don't you take a breather? You look beat," Tessa said laughing.

"It's not normally this busy. I don't know what happened," Rebecca said leaning against the counter.

"Well, I might have had a little to do with that..."

"Huh?"

"Aaron runs an RV park, you know. Well, I made some quick flyers this morning and he has been handing them out to his guests. A lot of these people are tourists," she said waving across the filled coffee shop. Rebecca's eyes welled with tears. She had never seen people who would rally around a perfect stranger like this before.

"Tessa, what a sweet thing to do. Please thank Aaron for me too. The extra income always helps," she said, not wanting to give away just how much it helped. "If you want to go now..."

"Oh, no. It's fine. I've kind of enjoyed this. I see why you love this place," Tessa said smiling. "Why don't you go freshen up. I know you must want to get out of those clothes you've been wearing all day."

Rebecca did want to get out of the clothes. She tried to avoid smelling under her arms until she was out of sight and halfway up the stairs. Yep, she needed a change of clothing before she scared everyone in town off.

As she went upstairs, she saw Leo sitting on the sofa watching music videos on his laptop. Curiosity about what happened at the island was killing her, so she changed her clothes and sat down next to him.

"Yes?" he said with a laugh as his mother stared over his shoulder.

"I was wondering if I could talk to you for a minute?"

"I guess so," he said in a typical teenage tone. Shockingly, he pushed the laptop aside and turned toward her.

"I've just got to ask... What happened today?" she asked, jumping straight to the point.

"What do you mean?"

"I mean that you hated Jackson Parker, and now you seem to be okay with him."

"He's not so bad, I guess," he said shrugging his shoulders.

"Leo, I want you to know that anytime you ever want to talk about your Dad, you can talk to me." There, she said it.

"Seriously?" The shocked tone of his voice broke her heart. Had he believed he couldn't come to her?

"Of course, honey. If I ever gave you the impression that you couldn't talk to me about your father, I'm so sorry. It was just so hard to talk about him, and I didn't want to bring it up and make you sad."

"Mom, I never knew him. It's hard to be sad about a man I never met. And when people talked about him, you seemed sad. So I stopped bringing him up."

"Is that why you've been angry lately?"

"I guess. Maybe. I mean, I see my friends with their fathers and I feel like it isn't fair that mine was taken. I might have taken it out on you, but I know it's not your fault. The worst part has been watching you, though," he said looking down.

"Watching me? What do you mean?"

"Watching you not have a life. Not have a husband. Not move forward. I felt stuck because you were stuck." The words coming from his mouth stunned her. He wasn't always the most eloquent kid, but what he'd just said was so telling. She reached out and hugged him close, and he didn't back away for once.

"Oh, Leo, I'm so sorry. You're right. I've been stuck for twelve years. I've been stuck on a day. One day out of thousands of days. That's not fair to you," she said through quiet sobs.

"It's not fair to you either, Mom," he whispered. She nodded into his shoulder, unable to speak.

After a few moments, she pulled back and quickly wiped her eyes. "Okay, what would you like to know?"

"About what?"

"About your father. Ask me anything," she said smiling.

"What did you love about him?" he asked crossing his arms and sitting back against the sofa.

"Wow, so many things... His eyes, his strong hands, his sense of humor, the way he took care of his little family, his sense of style, the way he made meatloaf..."

"Meatloaf?" Leo asked with a chuckle.

"Oh, yes, he made the best meatloaf..." she started, and spent the next thirty minutes telling Leo more than he'd ever known about his father. And more weight was lifted from both of their shoulders.

THAT EVENING, Jackson showed up at Jolt in his finest suit with a yellow rose in hand. He was going to do his very best to not allow her to say no to him.

It was Tessa who let him in since Rebecca was turned around cleaning off the counter. Jackson smiled at Tessa and walked around to stand in front of Rebecca. When she looked up, she appeared almost startled. Her face had a few beads of sweat, and her hair had fallen down into her eyes from a hard day's work. He actually found it to be cute, but like most women, she didn't appreciate a man seeing her like that.

"Jackson, I wasn't expecting you! You look fancy. What's the occasion?" She asked the question in between puffs. Jackson remained cool and collected as he handed her the rose, making her blush. Her fair skin always gave her away, and he loved it.

"I was thinking that I might take you for a nice dinner. Just the two of us."

"Oh, I don't know, Jackson. I mean, I'm not sure if I can leave Leo alone here." Leo came to back him up, just as he said he would. He must've been listening in because he came running down the stairs.

"Mom, it's fine. Jeremy wants to do a raid tonight, so I'll be on the Xbox anyway." Rebecca sighed and put her hand on her hip. The tension in the room was heavy as everyone realized Rebecca was about to come up with a new reason to protest. Luckily, Tessa swooped in and grabbed the rag out of Rebecca's hand.

"You go ahead and get ready, hon. I'll finish up here. You don't want to keep this handsome man waiting, do you?"

Jackson saw Rebecca glance back and forth between all three of them, and held his breath. This was the moment of truth.

She finally surrendered and smiled at him then headed up the stairs to get dressed. Leo gave Jackson the thumbs up before following behind her.

"You know, Tessa, I think I like you more and more every day. I should give Aaron a big hug for bringing you into our lives." Tessa laughed and shook her head before finishing up closing procedures.

In record time compared to any other woman Jackson had ever dated, Rebecca came tumbling down the stairs. She was a vision, her red hair down and straightened wearing strappy black heels and purple strapless dress. Her skin looked glowing in the now partially dark coffee shop, and he couldn't wait to have her on his arm.

REBECCA KNEW that she really should feel embarrassed and guilty that she'd allowed a complete stranger to run and close her coffee shop on a busy day and that she was now leaving her son alone for the first time since moving, but all she could think about was the handsome man sitting in the seat across from her.

He had brought her to one of the nicest restaurants in the area. She'd passed it a couple times and heard the locals talking about it, but of course, she'd never been able to afford to go. It was a high end seafood joint with décor all over the walls that definitely had an aquatic feel. The lights were dim, and the glass window at the back allowed for an unobstructed view of the beautiful ocean.

Luckily, the menu did not list the prices of the food because if it did, she'd probably have a heart attack and then insist on going somewhere more reasonable, but she was going to allow herself to enjoy something just one time.

The waiter came up dressed in black and white, and Jackson immediately ordered the house wine and an appetizer of shrimp scampi. For a moment it made her think of her husband. He'd been the exact opposite; totally indecisive. She made many decisions for him and her both because he was a very laid back and shy person. Jackson clearly was a take charge kind of man.

She silently told herself to stop comparing Jackson to her late husband, but it was easier said than done. Hopefully, their differences would prove to help her get away from that thinking.

Jackson smiled apologetically at her having just caught him ordering for them both. "I'm sorry. It's just a really bad habit I have. You're just so unlike the other women I've dated, and I wasn't sure if you'd like to order or not."

"Breathe, Jackson. It's not a big deal. It's nice not

making decisions sometimes, but just don't get the wrong idea about me. I'm no pushover." She pointed her finger at him in mock anger, and they both broke into laughter which they quickly quieted as the waiter came up with their wine glasses. She hadn't gotten to drink a lot of wine lately, but she loved it. Back in New York, before the tragedy, she and her husband had even belonged to a wine tasting group for a short time.

It was funny how she measured life in terms of the terrorist attack. Never as a little girl would she have imagined that she would have been caught up in one of the most infamous days in history, but here she was. Her life had been separated into "before the attack" and "after the attack".

Rebecca swiftly moved to place the napkin across her lap like everyone else in the restaurant. Ironically, even living right there near New York City, she hadn't spent much time in expensive restaurants. Looking around she felt dressed down compared to the others. She knew that wasn't logical since she was wearing her nicest dress, but she still felt out of place. This small town sure knew how to dress up.

When she looked up at Jackson he was smelling his wine, something she'd only ever seen people do in movies. She stifled a laugh as the waiter walked away, leaving the bottle at the table for them.

Jackson noticed her looking at him and got a little red in the face before taking a large swig of the wine into his mouth and sloshing it around.

His world was obviously so different from hers, and she wondered just for a moment why he chose her to date. It's not like Atlanta wouldn't be full of women that seemed more his type, but then again, he grew up quickly in a small, friendly beach town. Maybe city girls weren't really his thing. Which was probably unfortunate for him since he worked at a large business in the city. Rebecca found herself feeling suddenly very grateful and lucky that he'd spent so much time raising his siblings and then working. Otherwise, she probably wouldn't have a chance with this brilliant man because he'd be taken by now.

The waiter brought the shrimp out and asked to take their order. Jackson ordered for her again, asking for the ahi tuna. This would be a new experience for her since she'd never tried sushi or anything close before. She'd never really felt like spending that kind of time or money on something she wasn't absolutely sure she'd like. This was a night for indulgence, though, and she planned to enjoy it as such.

"So, tell me more about yourself, Jackson," she

demanded boldly. Jackson dropped the shrimp he'd been about to eat in surprise making Rebecca laugh.

"Well, what would you like to know?"

"Anything, really. I mean, it's a date, so we're supposed to get to know each other."

Jackson scratched his head. "Well, my favorite color is blue. Football is my favorite sport. I did terrible on my SATs, and I am a work-a-holic. Oh, and I love seafood." Jackson grinned mischievously and took a huge bite of shrimp.

"Well, I guess that's everything. So, the date must be over then," Rebecca responded jokingly.

"What about you? It's your turn."

Rebecca peeked at him from under her long eyelashes, about to protest. But, she decided to go ahead and play along. "Umm, my favorite color is emerald green. I don't really have a favorite sport. Does bowling count? I used to bowl when I was younger. I did so-so on my SATs, but the math portion really got me. I am a crazy, obsessive single mother of a troubled teenage boy, and I am more of a burger and fries kind of girl most of the time. Not that there's anything wrong with seafood." Embarrassed that she may have insulted his choice of food she cowered a little as she said the last sentence. There was probably no need to be worried though, since Jackson was beaming across the table from her.

"A woman after my own heart," Jackson replied making Rebecca's heart skip a beat. She knew he was probably making a joke, but the idea of it just made her feel butterflies throughout her whole body. It was weird how new relationships could make you feel and act like you were a kid again.

The waiter brought out their meals, setting two plates on the table with pinkish slabs of fish. At least, that's what it looked like to Rebecca. She tried hard not to make a face and offend Jackson or the waiter, but from the way Jackson was holding back a laugh she'd obviously failed. "I promise it tastes better than it looks," he assured her as the waiter walked away.

Forgetting her manners, Rebecca leaned down and sniffed at her plate making Jackson break out into full laughter. "Okay, just try it, and if you don't like it we'll go somewhere else for dessert." She nodded and grabbed her fork, wanting to stick to her guns and try something different. She pulled off a small corner piece and placed it in her mouth. She let it sit on her tongue a minute to give it her best shot, and mostly what she tasted was salty. The fish was okay, but the texture reminded her of a mixture of spam and snot. She quickly swallowed and smiled sheepishly at Jackson. There was no hiding her distaste.

Jackson sighed and looked at her but she was saved by her phone which began vibrating in her purse. She held one finger up to tell Jackson she'd be back and took off to the ladies' room, purse in tow.

Rebecca was surprised to hear Leo on the other end. "Hey honey, is something wrong?" She wasn't used to being away from him at night like this, and it worried her like any parent of a small child leaving them home alone for the first time.

"Everything's fine, mom. I just wanted to see if I could go to Danny's house. He just got a new game and wants to test it out. His mom said she could pick me up and drop me off, and I have the spare key for the shop." Rebecca contemplated for just a moment, wondering if that was a good idea. The truth was she really wanted him to build friendships in January Cove, and this was a great start even if it was based on video games. Plus, it would leave the apartment open for her and Jackson, just in case.

"Okay, sweetie, but please be sure to lock up and text me once in awhile to check in. Oh, and don't stay up too too late. I don't want your sleeping schedule to get out of whack for school." She could hear him sigh on the other side of the line.

"Yeah, mom. Thanks."

"Love you, honey."

"You too, mom."

Rebecca heard the click before she hung up herself and headed back out to the table. She was surprised to see that Jackson had already gotten the check and a to-go box for his meal. He smiled at her as she sat down. "So, madame, where would you like to go for dessert?"

Rebecca thought for a moment whether she should dare to invite him back to her place. I mean, she could just cook some burgers and scoop out some ice cream, and it would give them a chance to talk more casually. It didn't have to mean anything just because he was coming up to where the apartment was in the coffee shop, did it?

"I know just the place." She winked at him and took his hand to lead him to the car. She was going to take a leap of faith and jump right into whatever this was before it was too late.

CHAPTER 12

*J*ackson wasn't sure what to feel as he helped Rebecca haul in the bags of food she'd bought at the local market. She was clearly ready to have a more simple meal, and he was fine with that. However, he didn't know what kind of signal she was sending by inviting him into her home. He didn't even know if Leo was home or not, though he assumed the phone call she'd gotten was somehow related to that.

He followed Rebecca's lead up the stairs and couldn't help but take that moment to enjoy the view he had being behind her. She was a very naturally curvy woman, and she swayed just perfectly when she walked. She was so much more beautiful than the women he usually dated who were skin and bones really. He found that he preferred this more natural beauty to the beauty that came from surgery and piles of makeup.

The stairs led straight into a small living area with the kitchen at the back. It was cozy, but he noticed that someone in the kitchen would have a clear view of the television. That was a plus he didn't have at his rental in Atlanta.

He followed her to the kitchen as she flipped on the lights and began pulling out everything she needed to cook with. She was a woman on a mission, and for a moment she reminded him of his mother, a whirlwind in the kitchen trying to cook up a meal to satisfy all her boys. He let himself question why he ever thought what he wanted could be found in a place like Atlanta instead of his hometown. He knew right then where he was supposed to be, but he still wasn't sure how he'd get there.

When he noticed her tugging at her dress, he felt even worse about the date he had planned. He had made the mistake of planning a typical Jackson Parker date, but this woman deserved something so much less superficial than that. In fact, as beautiful as she looked in that dress, he could see it was not a natural state for her like it had been for his last girlfriend. This was a busy, working, single mother, and she looked and performed her best in something more practical.

He grabbed the pan out of her hands and pinned her up against the counter. For a moment he forgot what he was doing as he realized the heat between them in this closeness. He really looked at her up close, and with every flaw he saw he somehow liked her even more, all the way up to her freckles and blushing face. "Hey, why don't you let me start all this while you get into something more comfortable. You don't want to be cooking and eating this kind of food in that pretty dress." He saw her open her mouth to protest and decided to silence it, with a light kiss on the lips. She nodded in acceptance and took off to her bedroom to find something more suitable for the change of plans.

Jackson decided to get comfortable himself, slipping off his tie and jacket and placing them across the back of the couch. He also unbuttoned the top three buttons on his shirt for some more breathing room. Now he was ready to get his hands dirty.

He started looking through the fridge and freezer for some good sides to go with burgers and hit the jackpot - rocky road ice cream. He couldn't help himself as it had been a long time since he'd let himself indulge in something so simple. He turned on the burner to get it ready for the burgers, but his focus was on the ice cream. He searched the drawers for a spoon and chose the biggest one. Just as he went to dig right into the half full gallon of ice cream with the spoon, Rebecca came back into the kitchen wearing an emerald green shirt with some form-fitting black jeans.

He felt like a little boy who'd been caught with his hand in the cookie jar as she stopped in the archway and put her hand on her hip. He had been caught red-handed. "Do you always like to spoil your dinner with dessert?" He heard the harshness in her voice, but he could tell it was a game by the smile on her face.

"I just always thought that saving the best for last was overrated. Why don't you take a walk on the wild side and try some with me?" He pulled out a spoonful of rocky road and waved it in her direction. She quickly crossed the distance between them and went to pluck the spoon from his hand, but Jackson pulled it away and signaled for her to open her mouth. She did, and he guided the spoon slowly into her mouth as she sucked off the ice cream that was quickly melting.

She was turning redder by the minute, clearly feeling the tension between the two of them. As he took the spoon out of her mouth, she cleared her throat ready to get back to business, but Jackson was not ready for that. "You have some chocolate on your face, Rebecca." He pulled her into him, wrapping his arm around her waist, and went in to lick off the small dab of chocolate that was covering her left dimple. She was surprised and remained tense in his arms, but he wanted to make her feel safe and comfortable with him. He kissed her lips and neck and ears; anywhere he could reach. With each soft touch of his lips against her skin she seemed to relax into him more until she finally let go and allowed herself to kiss him back.

They spent the rest of the evening cooking, enjoying dessert and laughing. Jackson couldn't remember a time when he felt more at ease with a woman. It had been so long where he could be relaxed and act like himself, and sometimes he'd forgotten who he really was in the first place.

Rebecca was smart, sexy and sarcastic. She was funny, shy and outgoing at the same time. It was like God himself had created this perfect woman and dropped her right in front of Jackson, and he didn't want to screw it up.

When it came time to say goodnight, neither one of them wanted to.

"You know, you could stay... if you want," she said softly as they were saying goodbye at the door.

He thought about it. "I don't want to screw this up, Rebecca. I've made impulsive decisions that were a little too fast in my previous relationships."

"How about this - you sleep on the sofa and I'll sleep in the room. Tomorrow we can have breakfast together."

"And what if people talk? What if people assume something?" he asked, smiling as he leaned down and kissed her cheek.

"Then we'll let them talk."

CHAPTER 13

*J*ackson woke up to a phone call the next morning. "Hello?"

"Mr. Parker, it's John Marshall again. It looks like things aren't going to straighten themselves out here. The client's talking about backing out of the deal. There's protestors around the site. It's a mess."

Jackson sighed and sat up in the bed. He talked quietly so as not to wake Rebecca who was still sleeping in the next room. The clock on the wall said it was seven in the morning. He was so sick of his life being consumed by work. "Well, John, that's kind of a bummer. I was really looking forward to this deal, but with that much push back, perhaps it just wasn't meant to be."

He heard John start yelling across the line, but he just didn't care. "It's frustrating for all involved, John, but I think I'm going to cut my losses here. Also, I won't be available to take these kinds of emergency calls for much longer. I'll be doing some of my work remotely, so I'll be putting someone in charge shortly to deal with things like this." Jackson hung up feeling empowered. He should have stood up for his spare time so much sooner.

"Who was that?" Rebecca came waltzing in wearing a pink robe and rubbing her eyes. Apparently the phone call had woken her up.

"I'm sorry. I didn't mean to wake you."

Rebecca approached him to give him a peck on the cheek. "It's okay. I'm kind of hungry anyway. Plus, the coffee shop opens in a couple hours and Leo will be home."

Jackson pulled out his phone again and sent a quick text. He saw Rebecca giving him an inquisitive look and was glad when he got a reply almost immediately. "How would you like to see a Parker family breakfast? Mom's cooking a big one to celebrate the engagement before everyone has to go back to work. I'll have you back in time to open, okay?" Rebecca nodded, actually looking excited by the idea, and he gave her a love tap as she went to get dressed.

THE PARKER FAMILY house was abuzz with activity much like Thanksgiving, only some of the Parker kids were still in their pajamas. The table was already filled with eggs, bacon, ham, pancakes, and everything else anyone could possibly want for breakfast. Rebecca took a seat while Jackson got on the phone again. This time it was the Parker's landline, and his sister Addison had called to check in with everyone. Apparently, they were trying to convince her to come stay for awhile. She could see that everyone was concerned about the only Parker daughter, but no one was quite sure what was going on.

Everyone was chatting and enjoying their meal when a knock came at the door. Rebecca offered to get it since everyone else seemed busy with each other. When she opened the door she saw a thin girl, probably in her mid or late twenties with flowing brown hair and way too much makeup on for her own good. "Um..hi," the girl said, "I'm looking for Jackson Parker. Is he here?" The girl, who had a fairly thick accent, looked into the house and saw Jackson standing there on the phone. She blew past Rebecca uninvited and ran toward Jackson who was still on the phone. She heard the girl say something in another language, Italian perhaps, and then she froze. The girl jumped up and kissed Jackson straight on the lips.

The whole family at that point was staring in shock as the scene played out before them. "Addison, I'm going to have to call you back." Jackson hung up the phone, and Rebecca shut the door. Something big was about to happen, and her heart was hanging on by a thread as she watched.

"Roma, what the hell are you doing here? We broke up. How did you even find where I was?" Rebecca breathed a sigh of relief. This was a crazy ex come to haunt him. It wasn't fun, but it wasn't some big secret he was hiding from her either.

Roma went to grab a hold of Jackson's neck, and he swiftly removed her hands. "Oh, Jackson, I miss you. You know I have my sources." She smiled and kept stumbling all over Jackson. Rebecca wondered if she was drunk or just desperate. Pretty or not, she could clearly see why he had broken up with her.

"Roma, I really don't appreciate this. You see the beautiful redhead that opened the door for you? That's my girlfriend. This is almost my whole family here, and you just came barging in on a breakfast meant to celebrate my brother's engagement."

Rebecca saw Roma glare at her as she backed a couple steps away from Jackson.

"Oh. Well, we need to talk. Can we go somewhere a little more private?"

"If it will get you out of here faster, yes. You have five minutes." Jackson led her out the door past Rebecca, being sure to give her a peck on the cheek and mouth an apology to the on the way out.

Tessa came and grabbed her by the arm to sit her down with the rest of the family at the table. Mrs. Parker put some breakfast on her plate, and she started to pick at it with her fork. She was distracted, though, as she could hear an argument going on outside.

When Jackson came back in, he made a beeline for his mother and whispered something in her ear. Rebecca noticed she was pursing her lips. She turned around to see that Roma was sitting on the couch with her head in her hands.

After speaking with his mother he came up to Rebecca and led her outside. All of a sudden she felt very afraid of what he was about to tell her, and it turned out that it was with good reason.

"First of all I want to apologize for that. We hadn't really had the official conversation about past relationships, and this was not the way to find out about it. Roma and I weren't all that serious. She's actually a model, so she travels a lot. We were kind of off and on when she was in town, but her personality didn't mesh well with mine, so I broke up with her a couple months ago. She kind of gets the impression sometimes that she's the center of attention everywhere. Anyway, this is really hard for me to say but know that it's not definitely for sure yet. She kind of just sprung this on me... She says that she's pregnant, and that's why she tracked me down and came here." He pulled in a gasp of air as he finished.

Rebecca stood there for a moment trying to process what was just said. Her heart and stomach clearly knew because she could feel them drop to the ground, but it hadn't quite hit her head yet. She had no idea how to handle this. Just last night she was giving in to her heart because this man had given her reason to trust him, but was that all going to go down the drain now? Even if it didn't, what kind of life could they have together with her son and his child and his ex model girlfriend constantly running off to do photo shoots? "I think I'm going to walk home. Tell your mother thanks for breakfast, okay?" Rebecca took a deep breath and walked away from what might have been her future back to her coffee shop and troubled son; a representation of the single life she was doomed to keep living.

JACKSON TRIED TO FOLLOW REBECCA, but then he realized the mess that was waiting for him inside the house. Hopefully, Rebecca just needed some time to process and they could fix this later. Right now he had to figure out how a pregnant model ex girlfriend was going to fit into his life picture, especially now that things were becoming serious with Rebecca Evans; serious enough to uproot his job to stay with her.

Once he got back in the house, his mom was cleaning up in the kitchen with the other women, and the rest of the family had scattered to get ready to leave for home or work. He went to the living room and sat down next to Roma and saw that her mascara was running like she'd been crying. "Look, I understand how scary this must be for you, especially with your career and all, but let me make something clear. The relationship that I'm in is serious, and I have no intentions of ending it just because of this new revelation. However, if it turns out you are pregnant with my child I will be there financially and to care for the child. I'll be a good father to this child, if it's mine. That's all though. We aren't getting back together, Roma. Have you seen a doctor yet?"

"No. I've been afraid to let the press catch on to this. It could ruin me." Roma started crying again, afraid that her career was going to be over because of one mistake.

"Well, then, let's make an appointment here. I doubt the paparazzi is interested in January Cove. I'll go with you if you want."

Mrs. Parker came busting in on their conversation. "Jackson, I think she needs some rest. The girl's had a hard day. I'll call Dr. Korin and make an appointment. Why don't you give her some space and go sort things out in your own head? Roma, just go upstairs to the first door on the right. You can rest up in there, and we'll figure all this out later, okay?" Jackson hoped his mother's soothing voice would calm Roma's nerves for now, but he got the feeling his mother had an ulterior motive. That suspicion was confirmed as soon as Roma left the room. "I smell something fishy here, son. I've told you before about the pitfalls of dating these sorts of girls. They're dangerous. It could ruin what you have going with Rebecca. I mean, do you even know for sure that she's pregnant? She could be playing you."

"Whoa, Mom, slow down. The appointment will tell us, and I don't plan on this changing my relationship with Rebecca. However, I do have a responsibility if this child, if there is one, is my child."

"Look, son, I love you, and I'd like to trust your judgment. I just don't want you to miss out on the best thing that's happened to you in years because some money loving floozy wants to scheme to get you back. Just be careful, okay?"

Jackson nodded and decided to step out for awhile. He needed to clear his head and decide how to handle the situation. He had been planning on calling up to the office and arranging for a computer to be sent for him and an ad to be put up for a job listing for a manager. Then it dawned on him that Mark Tyner would be the perfect guy for the job. He knew Jackson well, and he certainly knew how to run the business. He had wanted to spend half his time working in January Cove so he could spend more time with Rebecca and Leo and have someone run things from the office for him. Like Kyle said, the business was built up really well by now, and he had plenty of people to take on some of his workload.

On the other hand, Roma was based in Atlanta, though she didn't spend a lot of consistent time there. When he thought about it, he really didn't even know what she'd do about traveling and her career once she was showing or after the baby was born. He got the feeling that he might be responsible for the child by himself while she went to photo shoots. In that case Atlanta wouldn't really be ideal. A small town was better for a nice, slow childhood, and he'd have plenty of help with childcare while he worked.

It looked like either way his plan to make his home base in January Cove might just be the smartest option for everyone involved.

Jackson found himself approaching Jolt without thinking about it. His heart had obviously led him there without him knowing. He glanced inside to see just a couple of customers standing at the counter waiting on coffee. Rebecca's back was to him, and he watched her make quick work of the drink orders, rushing around the counter. He could tell she was stressed by the way she was holding herself, shoulders and back completely stiff. If she worked all day like that she'd probably need a massage. Maybe that would be his way back in tonight.

Leo was sitting at a table in the far back corner,

on his phone like usual. Apparently he'd come home from his friend's house already. He felt guilty he hadn't talked to him in a couple of days now. He somehow felt responsible for this teenager that wasn't his, something that was really hard to handle when he supposedly had a child of his own on the way. He was beginning to understand why Rebecca had run off after the news that morning.

CHAPTER 14

*R*ebecca tried to smile as customers came and went, but she got the feeling she wasn't fooling anyone, not even her son. He had already asked her a million questions that morning after he got home and saw the mood she was in. He had since tried to get information out of her about how Jackson screwed up and was trying to convince her that she should forgive him. Leo was obviously as easily attached to this guy as she was, which made her feel even worse about what was going on. Could Leo afford to lose his male role model?

When her last customer walked out, she made the mistake of peeking outside. Just across the sidewalk she could see Jackson looking back in at her and Leo. He was afraid to come in, it looked like, and probably for good reason. He'd tangled himself up with the wrong girl and ruined the lovely evening they'd had. She was embarrassed that she'd fallen for the type of guy that would get involved with such an indulgent young girl and make a mistake.

She watched as he tried to flash a smile and wave at her, but she ignored it. She really couldn't afford to get in any deeper right now. It had already gone too far, and she wasn't really in the mood to discuss a plan about sharing a guy with a model and a brand new baby. Leo, however, did not have a problem waving back. This somehow led Jackson to the thought that coming into the shop was a good idea.

"Hi Rebecca." He cleared his throat.

Leo stood up from his seat and walked up to him to shake his hand. "Hey Jackson, what's up?"

"Not a whole lot buddy. Hey, would you mind giving your mom and me a moment?" Leo looked confused but nodded and went to man the register. Rebecca stood there for a moment not wanting to allow any excuses or pleading to change her mind about what was best for her and her son, but she felt bad that he was just standing there alone waiting on her.

She took a seat at the back of the shop as another customer came in for a simple cup of coffee. Hopefully Leo could handle it okay because she was probably about to get into the middle of something very difficult.

"Rebecca, I know how everything must seem right now. It isn't an ideal situation, but if she is pregnant, she's only a couple months along. There is no reason to make any rash decisions right now. We have no idea what she'll end up deciding to do. She's a model, a shallow one to be honest. She may not even want to be a mother. Can we just pretend like for now nothing has changed?"

Appalled, Rebecca shook her head. "First of all, I don't really like the way you're suggesting that you'd be okay with her aborting or giving up your child. I would hope that even if she wasn't mature enough to handle it, you would be."

"No, Rebecca, that's not what I was saying at all. Dang it, this has been a shock to me, so maybe I'm not expressing myself well. I would never want her to abort or give up my child. I'm just saying that she is very self absorbed, and she may get to make a lot of decisions that I won't have a say in. That scares the crap out of me, to be honest. Roma is not the person I would want in charge of a baby, especially mine."

"Let's be honest. You got involved with a young,

beautiful girl. You say she's shallow, but what does that make you if you got involved enough with her to get her pregnant? I am clearly not the right woman for you. You may feel excited now, experiencing something different, but you have a 'type' it seems, and that type is not me. Besides, if she does decide to keep it, she can offer you something I can't; a whole family. My family is broken. Leo is not your real son, and I will always love a man that's no longer with us, no matter how I feel about you. She's free to love you fully and give you your own child."

"Rebecca, I'm not in love with Roma. I *am* in love with you. I know it would be rough, but I feel like you are worth fighting for." Rebecca was floored by his confession of love. This was not how she pictured a man telling her he loved her; amidst a fight about him knocking up some model. She began to tear up, and she couldn't take it anymore. In her heart, she knew it was love, although she couldn't understand how it happened so fast. Was she being silly and immature herself?

"I'm sorry, Jackson, but I can't put my family through that kind of thing. I should never have gotten involved with you. Our lives are very different, and it just isn't a good fit. I had an amazing time with you, and I appreciate all you have done for us. I have a coffee shop to run now." She wiped her eyes and headed back for the counter without another word. She hoped he'd get the idea that he was dismissed so she could be free to break down the way she knew she would any minute now.

Luckily, with a tear welling from his own eye, Jackson slinked out of Jolt without another word.

"Mom! I can't believe you just did that! He told you he loved you, and you just let him walk away like that? Why did you even bring him into our lives if you were just going to chase him away?" Rebecca could hear Leo's voice crack as he yelled at her, and it broke her heart to know that he was holding back tears just as hard as she was trying to.

"I know you don't understand, Leo, but it's for the better. It's not the kind of life either of us would want."

"Mom, I understand perfectly. I heard you. I get it; some girl showed up and said she was pregnant with his baby. You know, mom, girls in the city did this all the time. They'd say they were pregnant to trap some guy. I've seen it on movies and talk shows. Sometimes, they were pregnant, but it was usually someone else's. She's a model right? She's probably a gold-digger."

"Leo! That's a terrible thing to say. We don't

generalize people just because of their profession..." Rebecca chided, pointing her finger at her son.

"Either way, you could chase her away instead of him. Whether you want to admit it or not, you love him too. Why do adults have to make things so hard?" Leo stomped his way up the stairs, and Rebecca tried to breathe and carry on with her work. Customers were starting to come in for the morning rush, and she had to pull it together.

WHEN JACKSON GOT BACK to his mother's house, another surprise was waiting for him. His sister Addison came flying at him for a hug as soon as he walked in the door. "Addison, I thought you weren't going to be here for another few days! What's going on? Is my favorite brother-in-law here?"

She elbowed him in the side. "You mean your only brother-in-law right? And no, it's just me this time. He's just really busy. I was actually on my way when I called this morning, but I wanted to make sure everyone was cool with it first."

"Why wouldn't we want you here, sis? We could always use another girl in the mix, right Mom?"

Their mother smiled as she walked past with a basket full of laundry.

"Well apparently I'm not the only new woman addition here. I hear that Aaron has a new belle and that you, sir, are about to get a family. That's so exciting, right?"

Jackson could tell by the smile and jumping for joy that she wasn't exactly clear on the details. "It's not really like that, Addison. Roma's my ex, and it wasn't even serious. She just kind of showed up here this morning and ruined breakfast and my relationship with an amazing woman. I was even going to move here for her. I'm not sure what Roma wants, I mean she's got plenty of money, and she doesn't really seem to be the motherly type."

Jackson realized looking at Addison that she was suddenly mad. "I would think you'd be a little more sensitive, Jackson. It takes two to get pregnant, and she's probably scared to death. She just doesn't want to be alone in this, I'm sure." Addison stormed upstairs. "I'm going to take a shower." Jackson and his mother exchanged confused glances as she slammed the door.

"What's going on with her, Mom?"

Mrs. Parker shook her head. "She just got here a few minutes before you did, and she hasn't said much. I think her marriage is a little on the rocks. She'll talk about whatever is going on when she's ready."

Jackson nodded and then heard a knock on the door. He went to open it to find Leo standing on the doorstep. This morning was really full of surprises.

"What are you doing here, Leo? I don't think your mother would want you to be here right now. Does she even know you left?"

Leo shrugged and stepped into the house. "I overheard the basics of what's going on, and she didn't like my opinion. We fought, and I decided to ride my skateboard here. I actually wanted to talk to you about it."

"I don't think that's a good idea, Leo. I mean, this is a pretty grown up problem."

Leo interrupted, "Don't give me that. I'm fourteen, not six. Plus, I'm from New York. This sort of stuff happens up there all the time. I'm here because I was wondering if the model in question happened to be Roma Maggiano, the Italian girl from Atlanta?"

Overhearing, his nosy mother came to sit down with them. She put her finger over her lips and then pointed upstairs, a signal to be quiet since Roma was right up there and might hear.

"Yes, that's the one. Why do you ask?"

Leo reached into his pocket and pulled out some folded up pieces of paper and handed them to Jackson. Mrs. Parker leaned forward to look over his shoulder. On the paper was a story printed from an Internet tabloid. It was clearly about Roma and showed pictures of her doing cocaine in the back of some club. The story was talking about how she was going broke buying drugs and had lost her last two gigs because she showed up high. Mrs. Parker ripped the paper out of his hands and started scanning the story again with wide eyes.

"Look, Leo, I appreciate what you're trying to do, but tabloids aren't really right all the time. They like to make things up and use photo manipulation to corroborate their stories. It makes them more money if it's something outrageous." Mrs. Parker didn't seem to be buying Jackson's doubts and made her way up the stairs to where Roma was staying, her lips pursed in a tight line.

Jackson knew that look meant she was on a mission and there was no changing her mind, so instead, he just followed her so he could be there to calm things down when the damage was done.

Mrs. Parker swung the bedroom door open like a mad woman to find Roma laughing on her cell phone and speaking with someone in Italian.

Without a word, she grabbed Roma's purse and dumped it out on the bed. Everyone gasped as a small bottle of Jack Daniels, half full, and a rolled up bag full of white powder rolled out onto the mattress. Roma's eyes went wide, and she hung up on whoever she was talking to. She was clearly about to plead or make an excuse, but Mrs. Parker beat her to it.

"So, you thought you could fool my family and use my son? You must be a really dumb woman. Your pretty face isn't going to save you here. Get out of my house before I call the police and report the fact that you brought drugs into my home!"

"But, I'm having his baby..." she pleaded in a thick Italian accent. She was squeezing her eyes in an attempt to produce tears on demand, but her tear ducts were not cooperating.

"Are you? Well, let me go get that home pregnancy test so we can confirm everything right now," Adele said as she started toward the door.

"No!" Roma shouted, and Jackson knew the answer. She wasn't pregnant.

"No? And why is that, Roma?" Adele said, hands on her hips.

"Um... I... Well, I may not be pregnant..."

Roma glanced at Jackson, looking for a savior,

but he put his head down and moved out of her way. Roma grabbed her stuff and scooped it back into her purse before running out of the door. She left the Parker house without a word, even as Leo yelled some choice words after her.

Jackson's mother made a motion like she was dusting herself off after some hard, dirty work, and turned to her son. "Well, don't just stand there. I believe you have a nice woman to win over. Now scoot." Jackson smiled at his mother's back as she went back about her business as if nothing happened. Leo held up his hand to give Jackson a high five, but instead Jackson went in for a hug. He was just so relieved that Leo of all people had helped him find a way out of this mess. He should've known Roma wouldn't dare be pregnant. And he wondered for a moment just how far she would have taken the fake pregnancy. The thought scared him a little.

"So how are we going to convince your mom to listen, buddy?" Leo thought for a minute then whispered an idea into Jackson's ear. "Well, then, I guess I'll see you tonight, Leo. Thanks again for helping a guy out." Jackson winked at him and walked him out. Leo's skateboard was sitting on the porch, and Leo hopped on it to skate back home.

Jackson ran upstairs to change. He had some

things he had to take care of, and he only had a few hours to do them in.

Rebecca had somehow made it through the day without unloading on a customer or having another fight with Leo. He'd gone for a ride on his skateboard for a little while that afternoon and came back in a better mood. Hopefully, she would be able to get her optimism back half as easy as her teenage son.

Now in the shower, she let the warm water distract her and work out some of the kinks in her stressed body. When she turned off the water she could hear music coming from the living room. Curious as to what Leo was up to, she quickly wiped down and pulled on some pajamas. She didn't expect it to be an exciting night. She'd probably read and sulk in the bed for a few hours before going to sleep.

When she stepped out into the living room, her eyes quickly narrowed. The music playing was Frank Sinatra, not something her son would generally be listening to. Out from the shadows stepped Jackson, dressed in some nice jeans and a polo, one of the most dressed down outfits she'd seen him in. She was about to tell him to get out of her house when Leo came out of his room. "Just dance with him, Mom. Do it for me." Leo and Jackson must have cooked up something together, and she didn't like the feeling that she was being manipulated. However, she also couldn't ignore the request of her son. She was just now able to communicate with him again, and she couldn't afford to ruin it.

Jackson held out his hand to her, and she set her face in a scowl but approached him and took his hand nonetheless. Leo disappeared back into his bedroom, probably to give them privacy. At least without him in there she could be honest and didn't have to pretend to be okay with this.

"So, now you're using my son to manipulate me?" Jackson looked offended by her question, and she almost wanted to take it back, but then again, she didn't want to give him the chance to toy with her either.

"Your son actually came to my mother's house today with some interesting information. It turns out that your teenage son knew more about Roma than I did." Rebecca found herself getting slightly curious. "He found an article about her in a tabloid that said she was losing money and contracts because of drug use. My mom confirmed that this afternoon when she searched Roma's purse. We assume she just wanted money. There's no baby, Rebecca."

As much as Rebecca wanted to breathe a sigh of relief, she wasn't sure she was out of the woods yet. The situation had really shaken her up, and she'd been rethinking the fact that she should get into a relationship in the first place. When Rebecca didn't respond, Jackson dipped her and smiled. "I have some other news too. I called the office today and talked to Mark, my assistant. He's going to step into a leadership position and help me learn to take time off and enjoy life again. They're going to be sending me a computer. I'll be looking for an apartment and moving some of my work here. I'll still have to go into Atlanta once or twice a month, but I'll be living here. I want to be with you and Leo, Rebecca."

As much as Rebecca wanted to protest and stay strong she just couldn't. She had been strong for too many years, and she just needed someone to count on and lean on right now. She fell into Jackson, forgetting about the music and the bad morning she'd had and just clung onto him for dear life. She began to cry and he just held onto her, rubbing her back. It felt so comforting, reminding her of the way she used to comfort Leo after he had nightmares when he was little. "I love you," she told him, and he whispered it back in her ear as they swayed back and forth to the music.

She just barely noticed Leo peeking out from his room, winking and giving her the thumbs up. She laughed away her tears and invited him in for a hug. For the first time in a long time she felt like she had a family, and she was happy. She hoped that wherever her husband had gone he was happy for her too.

CHAPTER 15

*A*ddison shut the door to her old room and looked at herself in the vanity mirror. It had been a long time since she'd been back in this room alone, since she usually visited during the holidays with her husband. She could tell by looking at herself that she looked different, like something was going on in her life, but she hoped that it was her paranoia.

Not that her mother hadn't already noticed that something was going on with her, and Jackson would probably sniff it out soon too. She hoped that it might be awhile since he had his own stuff to deal with right now. She was very happy for him, finally looking for a woman to be serious with. She'd secretly been worried about him for years, wondering if he'd ever find a serious woman and step away from his work long enough to have a family.

Thinking about the future he might have made her sad though, and she pulled out her phone to check it. As usual, there were no messages of any kind. Something about a cell phone not in use could really make a woman feel lonely.

She sighed and tugged at her shirt. It felt a little tight these days. She'd found herself gaining a little weight over the past few months, and her body didn't look quite like it used to.

She had once loved change, especially when she got married and moved to another city. Everything felt great and brand new with someone to share it with, but now she hated change. It made her afraid. She knew she should probably talk with her family about what was going on since they'd find out eventually one way or the other. She couldn't hide what was going on with her forever, but she just hoped to hold it off until after the holidays.

She wanted nothing more right now than to distract herself, and everyone else, with a fun Parker Christmas, an event the whole family came for every year.

But would her own problems end up causing drama she didn't want or need right now?

CHECK out Rachel's other books at www. RachelHannaAuthor.com.

Made in United States
Cleveland, OH
05 May 2026

36612371R10121